Love
Jude

Love
Jude

Annie Porthouse

Other books by Annie Porthouse:
Dear Bob

© Annie Porthouse 2004
First published 2004

ISBN 1 84427 044 0

Scripture Union, 207–209 Queensway, Bletchley, Milton Keynes, MK2 2EB, United Kingdom
Email: info@scriptureunion.org.uk
Website: www.scriptureunion.org.uk

Scripture Union Australia, Locked Bag 2, Central Coast Business Centre, NSW 2252, Australia
Website: www.su.org.au

Scripture Union USA, PO Box 987, Valley Forge, PA 19482
Website: www.scriptureunion.org

The right of Annie Porthouse to be identified as the author of this work has been asserted by her in accordance with the Copyright, Designs and Patents Act 1988.

British Library Cataloguing-in-Publication Data
A catalogue record of this book is available from the British Library.

Cover design by Phil Grundy
Printed and bound in Great Britain by Creative Print and Design (Wales) Ebbw Vale

Scripture Union is an international Christian charity working with churches in more than 130 countries, providing resources to bring the good news about Jesus Christ to children, young people and families – and to encourage them to develop spiritually through the Bible and prayer.
As well as our network of volunteers, staff and associates who run holidays, church-based events and school Christian groups, we produce a wide range of publications and support those who use resources through training programmes.

To Bunz, my real-life 'Bob',

whom I love,

lots.

Eggs going cheap

Thur 7 Apr

3:16 pm

Dear Bob

No no no... Dear Oren?

No... Dear Jude/me/self/diary?

In any case, have only been going out with Oren now for 10 days, 18 hrs, 16 mins, and, er, 26 secs... well, not that long really, so think will stick to writing to you, 'Bob' (my fantasy future hubbie-to-be), for the time being.

Life is hard, Bob – there are so many brain-taxing, mind-boggling, life-depending decisions to be made... Consider me right now, right here, perched on edge of my bed, gazing longingly at the sea of Easter Eggs laid out before me... but which one to devour next?

1] *Spider-man (complete with additional S Man figure)*?

2] *Barbie (pink lipgloss ring)*?

3] *Tweenies (multi-coloured Doodles watch)*?

All these freebies do rather distract from the choc itself – what Easter is all about after all.

Hmm... will opt for Barbie.

Told Oren, when we bought these in Woolies yesterday (cheap, as Easter now been and gone), that Barbie kinda depresses me, being so much babe-ier than me. He said he'd heard that if a woman were altered to have Barbie's exact bodily proportions, her neck wouldn't be able to support her head, and it'd snap instantly. This helped (and the fact that he pinched my bum while we were at the counter – who wants Barbie's butt when Oren is pinching MINE?!).

Yum city! Tastes divine. Wonder if heaven will consist of a billion billion reduced-priced E Eggs (of varying types), all spread out before you for eternity – yum.

Wonder if all those band/singer ones would get past Pearly Gates... Britney? Kylie? Busted?

Ooooh. Can hear convo from downstairs... will just open door a tad more...

Sorted.

My parents love Oren. Dad's just asked him how he came to be involved with Romania, and now Oren's off. For a bloke of few words, he's able to say an awful lot about the few passions of his life, and Romania is one of them. I can just picture Mum and Dad's faces now, eyes all lit up expectantly, absorbing everything they can possibly glean from their 2nd daughter's 1st b/f!

Still, it's sweet, I guess... is better than them hating him or something.

Hmm... who would be able to hate him anyway? He's perfect, pretty much.

Ahhh... now Mum's offering him a 'nice cup of tea'. No doubt she'll find an extra large saucer and perch some massive rock cake thing on it. She can't seem to stop feeding him. OK, so he's not exactly big/hunky/chunky, but he seems to get by on what he eats. No need to go overboard, Mum – like, he's not gonna waste away. He's not going ANYWHERE! He's mine now!

Oooohhhhh... big brain-invading thought of the day...

IS HE MINE??!

Post-10-min break to ponder (panic) I mean, we're 'going out' now, but what does that really mean? It was all so sudden, so romantic, so 'right' that have hardly given a thought to what HE'S thinking – about me, about us, about... the future.

After years of endless bloke-hunting, one finally hunts ME down and we get together... I should feel like everything's all sussed and sorted, and I did – up until a minute ago.

Arrrrggghhhhhhhhh!!!

Is he taking this seriously, or is it just fun? Like, not just *fun*, but just... just a 'relationship', which may or may not last – one of those 'wait and see how it goes' things? I mean, this is probably IT, isn't it?

Is he the bloke I've been waiting for – Mr Right – 'the one' – my future life-partner and all?

What if blokes, even Christian (Cn) ones, are in need of convincing that you're 'wife material' before they'll commit? I feel a mission coming on:

To ensure I'm the ONLY lass he'll ever want or need.

Must be top g/f. Must love him, support him, listen to him, etc etc.

Must must must.

Feel a bit better now – will go down and rescue him from potential rock-cake situation, and nosy, over-keen parents, and be really
Nice n stuff.

Sat 9 Apr

9:21 pm

Phew, well-knackering day.

OK, so journey back to uni wasn't bad (about an hour n a bit), but all that packing/emotional goodbyes/organising etc is all too much for a Sat. Sats are supposed to be relaxing/being slob-like in style of Homer Simpson. Still, didn't complain once to Oren – even helped him pack! Well, had only just started cramming stuff in his rucksack when he suddenly suggested I take Nat to the park, to give Abby a break (Eve hanging off her boob at the time). Sure he appreciated my help tho – packing is just one of the many many uses of a good wife... let's hope he picked up on my talents.

Ha! The park trip – that must be cause of my state of total knackeredness (real word? correct spelling?). Nephews, esp 2-year-old ones, are fast, busy, excitable, tiring creatures. Would have preferred to swap with big sis, Abby – at least she got to SIT and watch children's TV while she fed Eve (not sure if my boobs would be up to it tho – when we're with child, Bob, will my teenier-than-Mum's-rock-cakes sized boobs be ABLE to produce?).

Still, am back home now. Home? Well, back in this midget-sized room, property of Bymouth Uni, with waterproof curtains (yep – they're still there).

So, 3rd semester's coming up – funny to still be a baby fresher.
But at least am fresher with a BLOKE!

Am waiting for Liberty (aka 'Libs') to call round – wonder if she's thought any more about God and stuff, since Romania. Even if she has, not sure I'm the best candidate for, you know, 'witnessing' and stuff. It was ME, after all, who got all freaked out last Sept (when just started at uni) and 'lost' God altogether, then found myself on massive hunt for 'the truth' – only to eventually find that God WAS there and WAS the truth and DID think I was FAB (as opposed to big fat loser) etc etc (while I was in Romania).

Am sure there are others more suited to the witnessing thing, like Lydia – the best ex-CU president out there (one assumes), or her new hubbie Jon, or MY (probable) hubbie-to-be, Oren. Yeah, they can sort her out, should she have any remote desire to be sorted out, which is unlikely...

In the same way that me winning next year's Miss World competition is 'unlikely'.

Just read back over yesterday's letter: correction – Easter is, of course, all about Jesus, and not about choccie (whoops!). Additional thought re novelty E Eggs – forget Britney etc, heaven's shelves'll be well-stocked with Delirious/Tribe E Eggs, complete with free WWJD wristbands – can't wait!

Also, re today's reference to 'emotional goodbyes': was only Mum who was emotional, dabbing multiple layers of Kleenex (with extra balsam, whatever that is) at her eyes as she bid farewell to her only 2 daughters on the same day. Not sure I was emotional, tho it kind of brought a lump to my throat when I saw Dad place his hand on Oren's shoulder, by way of a goodbye, with a kind of take-care-of-Jude look about his face.

My 2 fave men, standing together, as if

Ah – door – is Libs – catch you later!

Mon 11 April

1:30 am (should be in bed) (oh, technically is Tue anyway)

Hmm. Not sure is good plan to stay up till 3 am when you're back to lectures etc the following day. Libs planted herself firmly on the beanbag in my room, after I'd come back from church with the others, and didn't move her rear until the aforementioned hour. Not that I wanted her to leave tho – we had great chat. Not v deep or anything, just, you know, stuff!

Had ½ wondered if she'd have come to church with us, but twas not to be. She doesn't seem to want to talk about God much, but I think that's coz it gets her thinking about the other big issue that's been on her mind recently, that she only told me about just before Romania – about the abortion, a couple of years back. Still, she says she might come to BURP (Bymouth Uni Revival Mission, our uni CU... in case it'd slipped your mind!) this Sat, and she does seem to be getting on OK with Fax (our new BURP president), since Romania, so we'll see.

Was great, no AMAZING, to sit in church yesterday, holding hands with Oren! Found it hard to listen to sermon – just caught up in the wonderment of no longer being a sad sad singleton, who can only gaze in awe and jealous-ment at the other couples in the cong (congregation). Keeping up my efforts to be awarded g/f of the year, I dashed off and fetched Oren his coffee at the end of the service, gave it to him… Then realised I'd failed to include bourbon with the deal, so dashed back to get one, only to realise that this week there was a CHOICE between bourbons and custard creams (assume church must have received large monetary donation over Easter hols) so dashed back to ask what he wanted, but he was yapping with Lydia and Jon, so dashed back and got him one of each (to be on safe side) and dashed back over to him, but made my approach just a little too enthusiastically, and managed to knock into his mug and shower him and several innocent passers-by with hot coffee!

He didn't look best pleased, but said it was 'no big deal'. Huh! A little word of thx would have been great for my marathon efforts in supplying him with refreshments, but I didn't comment – good g/fs are HAPPY to serve their blokes, whatever the cost, and for no thx whatsoever (aren't they?).

Lectures OK, if rather yawnyawn.

Main thing to report today is that started at Fusion (Bymouth nightclub). Libs kindly got me on the rota, as she works there too and seems to have a stack of responsibilities, which is not a word normally associated with our Libs!

Crazy? Yep. Wild? Yep. Bloke-mad? Yep… Responsible? Hmm… nope.

Anyhow, she's sorted me out with 12 hours a week, 9 pm – 1 am, Mon, Wed and Thur.

Job involves the mind-numbing task of collecting empty glasses from tables (and loos/stairs/floor etc) and returning them to the bar, washing and drying them, ready for use again. Was well-nervous – not re the actual task in hand, but just coz I don't know the other staff, and couldn't help thinking they were all staring at me, thinking:

'Ahhh. There's the new girl, she's… rubbish/slow/ugly/fat etc.'

Worse thing was seeing them chatting together, looking in my direction. Got a bit freaked and gave myself 30 second break to go see Libs:

Me: Libs, the others aren't all thinking that I'm pathetic, or talking about me behind my back, are they?
Libs: Yes, doll.
Me: Huh?
Libs: They ARE, but in a few weeks you'll have got to know them all, and

it won't happen… well, it won't happen as much as it is now, babe, so chill!

Surely a better friend would've just lied, eh?

So, tonight/this am have earned… ummm… £6 x 4 hours = £24 = not bad!

Will end now so can text Oren – yes, is v late, but he won't mind – I am his super-amazing-do-NO-wrong-babe, after all!

Tue 12 Apr

4:31 pm

Fell asleep during Prof Carr's lecture on 'controversial applications of psychological research' this am. No, is not just figure of speech – I actually did, in the sense that my head fell forward, and just woke up in time to save myself from it coming into contact with desk, which was most fortunate. No one noticed. At least, this is what am telling myself. How Libs works so much, and so late, will never know. She must be super-human, but in a student's body. Cool.

Saskia, my best BURP-buddie, just rang me to discuss next year's HOUSING situation! I'm like, 'Hey Sas – it's only April!' But apparently it needs to be sorted soon-ish, so better get bum in gear re the whole business.

Housing-related questions, in no order of importance/stress-ness:

1] *Who do I want to share a house with? Oren?! Like, he's my man, but is it OK to live under same roof with him, from a Cn viewpoint?*
2] *Where in Bymouth do I want to live?*
3] *Cost? And will I have to work all hrs at stare-city Fusion just to afford rent?*
4] *How will I cope without a cleaner to come and 'do' my room on regular basis?*
5] *How will I cope without Mr NextDoor (the hash cookie-making, plump, yet friendly, M Manson lookalike)?*
6] *Will a real house feel less like living in a Butlins chalet than now?*

Hmm. Is all a mystery. Will have to discuss with Oren – he'll know what's best. He's so good like that.

Think I love him.

Sorry, know that was a bit sudden, and not on topic of 'housing in Sept' but I really think I do!

He's the best person I know, I can't stop thinking about him, I fancy the pants off him (tho not literally, of course) and, when all's said and done (stupid over-used, yet awfully handy, expression)... yep – I want him for keeps!

Still being v v nice/kind/helpful/polite etc when in his presence. Think it's doing the trick, but can't be sure. Perhaps should ask his mates what he's saying about me, or is that too obvious/sad/desperate etc?

Don't think should be stressing re housing *and* 'love/future with Oren' in same eve... is not good for underused brain... will go get some Pringles (pizza flave) from my kitchen cupboard, and R E L A X !!

Oooohhh... text from Sas.

Nooooo waaaayyyy.
Duncs n Lauren have split up!
Will ring her for more info (I mean, er... to learn more re situation, so I can pray for them).

Wow – they actually split up whilst AT Spring Harvest! Bizarre – wouldn't think such a thing as splitting up with one's partner was possible on such holy ground! Sas says that Duncs told her he ended it... but that Lauren said it was totally 'mutual'. Perhaps he's still lusting after me, like he was last Sept, until his soulmate and partner in geek-i-ness caught his eye... then it was bye-bye Jude, and hello lushious Lauren (although she is, clearly, far from being this, but love is blind and all that).

Feel dead sorry for them both... detect that Sas gave me rather too much info than can qualify as being 'for the purposes of prayer', bless 'er. Both parties are well-depressed, she says. Well, twas obviously not meant to be. Still, we'd kind of all assumed they'd be together for good – like, who else would want to take either of THEM on!

Arghh – now am thinking about me again (surprise, surprise). Like, just coz me and Oren seem all couply and 'as one', could a 'romantic-weekend-away-at-major-Cn-conference-resulting-in-him-dumping-me' be just round the corner?

Weekend away aside, is it just poss that he could be all 'adios Jude' when I least expect it, and will I then have to go around saying that the split was all 'mutual'?
Huh?
Will I?!

9:23 pm Just occurred to me that still have those sex books of Oscar's in my room.

OK, that last sentence sounds really bad, like am porn freak or sim, but in actual fact it was all due to big mix up, and nowt to do with innocent little me (well… not much).
Have managed to stop myself from looking at them, so far.
OK, so have b/f now, but we'll be saving 'it' for the big M, as is the Cn way. I assume.
No, course we will.

Oren's not sex-mad or anything, is he? Do sex-mad people make it obvious that they are mad on sex, like Libs for example, or is it poss to be sex-mad and not talk about it, but then get a g/f and expect it once a night and twice on bank hols?

He's not mentioned it yet, and our snogging hasn't exactly gone on for hours or anything. Hmm.

Ahh – just thought that really ought to encourage Libs to see counsellor, re abortion (but not Oscar). There must be a normal, helpful one on site somewhere.

Perhaps will hold on to books for little while longer, just in case O (Oren, NOT Oscar – yuk, nasty mental image…) and I get married this semester and virgin Jude needs to find out some vital info before wedding night! (Tho guess Libs would probably be able to fill me in on the basics…)

Fri 15 Apr

1:25 am

Men!
Will warn you now, Bob, am not the happiest of bunnies.

Why? Firstly, am v tired, as just finished at Fusion (was packed, mainly with students with nothing better to do than to dirty glasses so that I have to go and collect them; then watch me as I wash and dry glasses; then order more drinks, dirty glasses again, and on and on and on, till 1 am).

Secondly, when tired, is not nice to have so-called b/f get all weird on me, just when things seemed to be going so well. He met me after 1st lecture today, and we came back here for a bit, before he had to go to his. Had thought he'd looked a bit serious from minute I saw him, but passed it off as nothing – he's generally a serious kinda bloke, after all. But, after general chit-chat (errr… and nice little snogging sesh, about which he didn't seem as enthusiastic as usual) he started saying that I've been a bit weird lately! Huh? Nearly went off on a wild one, saying that he knew what he was letting himself in for when he 1st came on to me, and it was a bit late now to back out etc etc… but instead I took a deep breath and counted to 10 (like people say you should do, to prevent going off on a wild one).

Remembered my 'being nice' plan, and also how much I liked/loved him, so remained calm, and asked him to explain himself further, as I was interested in what he had to say, as perhaps I could benefit from his wisdom on the subject of my character, and change myself for the better (wow – I'm good!).

But here comes the worst bit… he almost raised his voice to me (tho not quite) as he jumped up from my beanbag, with:

'That! That! THAT!! That's EXACTLY what I'm talking about! This past week you've been oddly nice and polite, caring and helpful, whenever we're together. Like just then… you were about to lose your temper and yell at me, but then you got that weird look on your face again, and went all… nice! It's just… it's just… well it's not… it's not YOU, is it?'

And with this he flopped back down on beanbag, ripped open a nearby packet of Hula Hoops (cheese flave) and began to deposit them rapidly in mouth, about 4 at a time… assumedly to regain energy used up from his little outburst.

OK, so you and I know about my reasons for being extra-nice in his presence – I only had the best motives, did I not? Not so easy to explain to him tho. Ended up saying that I was just v happy to have him as my bloke, and wanted to please him, but that I'd try to be more 'normal' in future, if my being kind/helpful/generous etc freaked him out like this.

Granted, I said it with hint of bitterness in voice, but he clearly didn't pick up on this – came straight over to me and gave me big smack-a-rooney on lips, and said 'thx'. Nice to have kiss from guy I love and taste of cheese H Hoops all in one swift move… yum!

Secondly, work itself wasn't exactly a laugh a minute. Still lots of staring from other staff, tho poss slightly less than before, but could just be wishful thinking. AND, in my enthusiasm to get about 7 used glasses back to bar in one go, I did the inevitable… ssssmaash! The sound of breaking glass is not pleasant at best of times, but when it increases staring from staff and punters alike 100-fold, is really not good. Why can't they just serve B Breezers and other such alcopops that don't need glasses?

Oooh – text – must be Oren.

Nope. Was Fax to inform me that, when glass breaks, the cracks move at speeds of up to 3,000 miles per hour. Now, Fax is pretty much 'in tune with the Lord' (is new BURP president after all) but somehow I suspect that Libs must have told him re my incident. Hmm… this means she's seen or been in contact with him since I am, no… 1:30 (she locks up and stuff). They sure are getting on well.

Ah, think I've done 2 'secondly's – whoops! Like I said, am totally knackered. Must get out of habit of writing to you this late. Sorry to be so down, but now am lost as to what to do re 'keeping' Oren, on permanent basis. And also feel crap every time I think about my new job.

Huh – why can't everything be simple and fun, as per primary school, huh?!

Sat 16 Apr

7:02 am

Woken up ridiculously early this am (6:28 am) – lots of shouting coming from outside. WHY?!
Have just managed to drag myself from comfort of bed to desk, so can let you in on what's been floating round my head for past ½ hour…
Oren. Or more specifically, how on earth I'm supposed to hold on to what we've got, now my 'being nice' plan has been rumbled.

Anyway, think I've found the answer – yeah!

When we 1st went out, he said he'd known, when I 'found' God for myself again, that I'd be all out for God – 100% like. I AM all out for God, I guess, but what if his definition of 'all out' and mine are different? What if he'll only marry someone who's as 'all out' for God as he is? Huh?

My only hope is to be a 100%-er, while managing to remain a SC&O (Sour Cream & Onion) flave Pringle Cn, like Oren, and a few of the other BURPers, in the hope that he'll notice and appreciate this.

No – don't accuse me of faking it! This isn't about being fake, as I really do know God now – we're good mates and all that, since what happened in Romania. But I just want Oren to know that am on his level, when it comes to… things of a spiritual nature. I just want to reassure him – that's not wrong, is it?

Will ponder on how exactly to do all this... just after a few more hours sleep, as shouting seems to have died down now.

4:32 pm I am in LOVE!
Have found what satisfies like no other.
Roasted salted cashew nuts!
(Almost as good as Soleros!)

Discovered them this am at Tesco. Well, assume they've already been 'discovered' in the sense that they are a product on Tesco's shelves, but have not personally sampled the delights that they offer ever before. They are soooooooooo scrumptious! Filled with a billion calories tho, but my new train of thought says that super-SC&Os (like myself) are not concerned with their outward appearance, and so can stuff their faces as much as they like (or is that gluttony or something... or is that sheep meat?).

Have run out now (despite bag supposedly containing 30% extra) so popping out to get some more supplies in. Then can treat the guys to some, when they come back here for post-BURP gathering.

Post-BURP/3 more bags cashews (Please note – that's 3 SHARED bags cashews!) Good to be back at BURP. Oren did it on our Romania trip. He said how well it went, but that he's suggesting changes to the way they do things at his home church, re the next trip they do. Something about us not being like Santa, and just giving them stuff/decorating schools etc, but enabling the Romanians to do things for themselves, and all that. All sounded v cool – think I probably had a v ha-that's-my-bloke look on my face for most of it, but don't care!

Discussion then got on to world poverty in general, and in a flash was reminded of Reuben (coz he went on about fair trade for a while. Amazing how quickly you can forget someone you spent 2 semesters totally obsessed with, innit?!). And then realised that he wasn't actually there... perhaps he's got yet another new lass and is out with her tonight. Don't care really.

Had really hoped Libs would come this eve, but she said she had stuff to do, which is prob just her way of saying,

'OK, so I was a bit interested in God in Romania, but now we're back and I couldn't care BEEEPing less.'
(BEEEP = word my mum wouldn't use, or even know!)

Called in on Libs after last person had left my room (Oren) to complain that have nothing to read now have finished that Vic Becks book she got me for my b'day. She has kindly lent me her copy of Robbie Williams' *Someone, sometime*. Not really my cuppa (tho do fancy him a tad), but will resort to reading it should I ever be free of assignments (or if I just choose not to do them).

Saw the Prozac packet by her bed, next to her fags… wish I knew how to help. What would a super-SC&O do for someone who's had an abortion/is on medication for depression/refuses to see a counsellor/won't even come to BURP?

Hmm. World poverty and all that… is real bad. Romania made me see the world differently. Am sure that while I was there I vowed to be wise with my money – never buy what I didn't need, give lots to the poor etc for evermore, but don't think have done any of this. Such noble thoughts got lost somewhere between here and there – on plane home perhaps? This is quite likely – people are always losing things on planes… will write to BA tomorrow and complain.

Must show Oren am as keen as he is re all this. Should I stop buying the edible treats I enjoy on occasion (errr… live for) and give the money I save to Romanian orphans?
Perhaps am not up to all this – have little (no?) desire to do this…
Am I 100% shallow and self-centred, rather than 100% all out for God? Hmm.

A fast day

Sun 17 Apr

Church (Bymouth Baptist) – sermon was on fasting. V interesting. Is important way to get more 'in tune' with God...

Sounds like important way to win brownie points with Oren to me! Not that I wanna do it JUST for him, as getting on better with God would be cool outcome too, but sure Oren will be well-impressed with such an act of... Cn-ness.

Yeah – will do it tomorrow... shouldn't be too hard – is only for a day after all.

Almost messed it all up by telling Oren I was gonna do it, then remembered, just in time, that big part of it is doing it in secret – is more holy that way, apparently. Will let him know about it somehow, obviously, but in a way that looks like he's found out by accident – yeah, cool.

Told Oren I'd go to evening service with him (he always goes, but the rest of us tend to pretend it doesn't exist). He was surprised, but seemed pleased. Qqqqqq

Sorry – just noticed how dirty my 'q' key was, and scratched dirt off it, thus creating a line of qs. Why do I feel compelled to share this sort of stuff with you, Bob? Coz it makes you seem real, I guess. ARE you Oren?

9:03 pm Just got back. Oren here, but in loo, so am typing this super-quick. Service OK, but only about ½ cong bothered to turn up, the bunch of skivers!

Oohhh... flush...
He's done... better go!

Just past midnight Hmm... OK, so technically is actually Mon now, but it FEELS like it's still late on Sun, so will just have a tiny snack now, to keep me going thru the day of fasting ahead of me... 1 bag cashews, 1 mini-tiramisu, 1/3 packet BBQ Pringles (left over from Sat eve) and... ahh – here it is in my wardrobe – my only remaining E Egg (*Spider-man*).

Yep – that ought to keep tummy stocked up for a day, seeing as have already eaten about 3 times as much as usual today, just to be on safe side.

Does it make me MORE or LESS spiritual to plan ahead in such a way? (You don't have to answer that.)

Mon 18 Apr

9:28 am

Fasting will help me lose weight, won't it? Surely such a deprivation of calories will shed a few pounds...
Or just a pound
or ½ a pound.

ANY loss would be fab really. Am off to lecture soon – feeling good... almost ate bit of Yorkie bar (that Libs just offered me when she popped by), but remembered in time and politely refused, much to her surprise.

11:48 am Would normally be thinking about lunch now, but is fine... no lunch is fine... Will have a bit of a pray instead – is what it's all about after all, innit?

11:53 am Hmm... that didn't last v long. Not coz I wasn't trying, but coz tummy is just beginning to make pathetic little rumbly noises... while heart and soul are saved, stomach clearly is not.

12:04 pm Does chewing gum count as food? No – course not, as doesn't get swallowed... will have some now.

12:08 pm Have just spat out, as figure that am still swallowing the juices of it, or whatever... sure that's not allowed (wish they covered this kind of stuff in N Testament/church sermons).

1:35 pm Don't think have lost any weight yet, and tummy turning up volume on those rumblings now. Still, only another... 10 hours 25 mins to go (I CAN eat at midnight, can't I?).

1:42 pm Just rang Sas to ask her re not eating (for whole day) and weight loss. She said something re the 'starvation response', and how not eating for a whole day could actually cause you to put on weight, rather than lose it!!

Wish I hadn't asked. Still, at least know am doing this for right reasons now, and not just for selfish improvement-of-body-image reasons.
Will be seeing Oren in couple of hours – can't wait for him to find out!!!
Am getting seriously hungry now, but will read Bible to take mind off it.

2:12 pm Getting into Psalms a bit now... let's see...

Honey, wine, manna, fatted calves, bread, fish… there's a whole lot more food in the Bible than you'd think… even those locusts are sounding tempting at this moment in time…
I AM HUNGRY!!!

5:49 pm Bad news – Oren just texted to say he's busy, can't see me now, but will collect me from work. Know I should be grateful, as good of him to stay up this late and walk me back, but REALLY wanted him to know about fasting thing asap. Huh.

Tummy now screaming at me for locusts…
on skewers with mushrooms/in sarnies.
Locust trifle anyone?
Now, what would Jamie O do with locusts?

8:45 pm Not sure if will live to see tomorrow.
Am soooooo in need of nourishment
too ill/weak/close-to-death to pray
need a Solero… need cashews.
Gimmeeeefooooddddddddnooowwwww!!!!!!!!!!!

2:02 am Good news – am well fed and feeling normal again (well, as normal as I am capable of getting). CRAP news – hmm, where to start?

Right, well am now convinced that working at Fusion is not conducive to fasting. (O taught me 'conducive' today – figure that, if he teaches me a new long word + meaning every day, I'll be almost up to his level of vocab in say… 3 years!)

Feeling weak etc does not contribute in positive fashion to rushing around in dark, noisy, crowded, mingin' club… trust me, I know. By time it was all over (is 4 hour shift, but swear tonight it felt like at least 8) and saw O standing at door to collect me, seriously began to question it all – was fasting really nec to let O know how spiritual I am? How close to death ought a g/f go to ensure she keeps her bloke? Vision blurry (even with glasses on) and found myself holding on to nearby chairs in rather desperate staggering way, en route to door/O. Had it really only been 24 hours without food? Not whole week? Huh?

Hadn't been able to grab any food whilst working, so 1st words to O were:
'Food – me – now!'

Whilst in McDs, he raised his eyebrows at my heavily stacked tray. Told him I hadn't eaten much today. Then paused and added:

'Well, to be honest Oren, I haven't eaten at all. I've been... well, you know... but we don't need to discuss it, let's change the subject.'

But he didn't. He was not impressed. Said that looking all weak and ill was not honouring to God, and to fast on a day you've got lectures AND work etc... he couldn't have been less impressed if he'd tried. He didn't really have a go or anything, but I could tell. You can always tell with him.

All that hunger and suffering for nothing... NOTHING. (Errr... apart from some extra prayer time/Bible browsing – goes without saying tho, dunnit.)

Wed 20 Apr

9:35 am/mid-read

Ha! So Robbie's secret fetish is...
playing Uno?!

A kids game, no less. Odd. You'd kind of expect him to be all drink/drugs and the rest. Book says he WAS like this once, but is now reformed, and would rather pass the time while on tour playing Uno with the rest of the band. Hmm. Deep.

How do you play Uno anyway? Is it hard/fun/really appropriate for famous music artists?

7:52 pm Just got back from long-overdue visit to Abby's. Took O along. Like my parents, Abby and Amos are crazy about him too – think they were more excited to see him than me! (Not that he should feel too privileged or anything – Abby told me that any visitor is a matter of much excitement when you're stuck at home for most of day with baby and 2-year-old.)

Abby seemed pretty good tho – since all that post-natal depression stuff, she's pulled through v well. Amos is really enjoying his new job with autistic adults... says he doesn't miss being stuck to computer all day one smidgen!

Ooohhhhh...
Can feel freaky pangs of jealousy creeping up on me, re 'the-perfect-Cn-household' situation...
Am so used to being jealous of my sis and her life that is hard to recognise sometimes.

Still, is not so bad since Eve came along and it turns out that Abby IS actually human, and does find stuff hard (Eve still not comprehending the whole 'night = sleep' idea).

Anyway, at least THIS sister has something to show off about now – her fab new bloke!

Only 1½ hours till work… bummer.

Sat 23 Apr

Whoops… Robbie's book is not called *Someone, sometime*, as stated in previous letter, is called *Somebody someday* (please don't sue/tell Rob… was easy mistake to make).

Thur 28 Apr

5:21 pm

Went straight to O's after lecture.
Was cool (being at O's house, not the lecture). Student houses are cool – can't wait to be in my own in Sept! That reminds me, must get that organised asap.

Watched a lot of SKY there, as not much else to do, and O wanted to get on with an assignment. Nice to watch him write/think/chew end of pencil etc. He's good to watch. He's good to kiss too, but enuf of that.

Ended up quite hooked on some holiday channel. Is mean how they put adverts for loans in the breaks, so that people get all fired up about having ace holiday abroad, then realise they can't afford it, then gasp in amazement as all their dreams have potential of coming true during commercial break. Shouldn't be allowed. Wanted to share this with O, but didn't want to disturb him… so just sat there and dreamed of where he and I could honeymoon instead!

When his assignment all done, we had good chat. I mentioned about the Rob book (Robbie is known as 'Rob' to his mates, so there!) and about Rob's past alcohol problems. O then said stuff about his dad – about his alcohol-related problems, how it affected O growing up, and his mum, and how it got his dad landed in prison.

V weird to actually KNOW someone who's in prison (well, to know his son, anyway). Don't give a lot of thought to fact that people actually are in prison, while we walk around all free and in charge of our lives etc. O is so strong – people who have naf upbringings always seem to turn out v strong, or v weak, in my opinion. I had v boring upbringing – nothing to report really. Perhaps is why I'm not strong like O – never really had to do much for myself, or think deeply about life, or take on board tons of responsibility before my time, and so on.

We tucked into a left-over black forest gateau that his housemate had said he could have. O insisted I take home remaining slice, to have on my own later… so I wouldn't forget our evening together (as if!). House had distinct lack of tupperware-type containers, so used empty Pringle tub to transport it in. Gave it a good wipe over 1st, but not convinced it was for the best – have shoved in kitchen fridge (the one here) as still full from 1st innings.

Do they get to have gateau in prison? Any pud at all?
Don't like thinking about prison really.

Sat 30 Apr

You know when you're so tired you're actually PAST being tired, and have moved into some whole other world where things are going on around you as normal, and you're there in body, but not actually there in mind, coz your brain's asleep, or trying to sleep?

Well, that's been me the past few days. Not sure this whole Fusion thing's gonna work out. Would be OK if didn't have lectures/assignments/revision do to. Perhaps should quit degree, but then would just be a normal person, living in student accommodation, working nights in a club… how long would it be before they'd find out and evict me? Hmm.

BURP good/challenging. Fax did it – picked up on what O had done the other week re world poverty etc. Pity he didn't TELL us he was doing this, as I'd have answered his opening question differently. He began by asking us whether we considered ourselves rich, poor, or somewhere in between. I said I was in between, but bordering on 'poor' (everyone knows students are poor). Also that my parents aren't poor, as in they don't sell the Big Issue on street corners… but then they're not rich, as per Mr R Williams. So, in between really, probably was my answer.

Knew something was up when spotted O rolling his eyes and placing head in hands. Huh?

So, yeah… thus followed Fax's detailed account of the world and it's distribution of wealth etc. Did you know that we are in the world's 20% richest, and yet we consume 86% of the world's resources?

Sas' mobile went off at one point, rather interrupting what he was saying, but he remained calm, and informed us that 90% of the population have never made a phone call.

NINETY PERCENT??!!
That's unreal.
Brought back all those deep and life-changing thoughts I'd had in Romania.

Ought to have quick pray re what I should do... hard to think that anything can ever really change tho, just coz a few people change their brands of coffee and all.

Right, will settle down to pray whilst eating this gateau that have just extracted from fridge, stored in Pringle tube, left over from Thur eve. Should be alright/not poisonous, eh? Has been in fridge after all. Will try it now...

Mmm... tastes fab, but has distinct BBQ tang to it (was BBQ Pringles tube). Think it actually improves the flave tho – is quite exotic (not that have ever been anywhere exotic or eaten actual exotic food). Will contact Jamie O – he ought to know about such developments in the culinary world (ie storing left over gateau in BBQ Pringle tube for 4 days). YUM!

Mon 2 May

8:05 pm

Really ought to be thinking about getting organised for work, but wanted to chat with you for a bit 1st – stuff on my mind and all that...

It's this whole 'being in a Cn relationship at uni' thing. Guess is different to having rel outside uni, in real 'grown-up' world. For example, when me and O 1st got together, most BURPers were well-excited for us. In contrast tho, several non-Cn mates have been more confused than excited – they can't get head round the fact we're not sleeping together. Hmm.

Sometimes get impression that they're just waiting for me to slip up and... sleep with him. Seems like everyone feels they have some kind of right to scrutinise my rel with Oren – the rel I've waited for all my life.

Take yesterday at church. Lauren had 'a word in my ear' during coffee, just when I was busy thinking that they ought to replace plates of biccies with bowls of cashews (roasted/salted). She said I ought to consider spending less time on my own with Oren, and replace it with time 'in a group' that he's a part of.

Like, am I allowed to SIT next to him? Look? Chat? Hold hands?

Actually, she had thoughts on that one too – she continued (which was odd as I had clear 'you're odd and you're scaring me' look plastered all over face) by saying that her and Duncs didn't kiss properly (whatever THAT means) for 1st 2 months of their rel.

WHY?!
Huh?
Is she suggesting I do the same? What, do we repent of the 'proper' kissing we've done so far, and pretend it never happened?

As soon as the crazy-lady (hey – she's just split up with her partner-in-all things-geeky, Duncs – who's she to talk?) let me go, ran it all past Lydia, who just laughed and said I was old enuf to know what to do in my own rel.

Kind of reassuring, esp as coming from de-throned (but always a saint in my eyes) CU pres, who actually went out with someone (Jon) AND married him AND they're still happy… but still, is my 1st ever REAL rel. Perhaps I would be wise to listen to such pearls of wisdom as Lauren's… will consider for a min.

Well, has been all of about 14 secs… and conclusion is…
Naaaaaaaa!

Must prepare self for work now… it comes round so soon – seems like EVERY eve for some reason, when is actually only 3 eves per week, innit?

Can't help but think ought to be revising instead… exams start nxt week after all. Trif.

Ha – cherry on cake (in bad way)… ER just starting and is v fab episode (the one where Romano's arm gets lopped off by a helicopter) and CAN'T see it as have to go to work. Bummer.

BTW, am not blood-thirsty in any way, just in case you're worried… but the way his arm flies through the air and the blood spurts ou

OK. I'll stop.

Thur 5 May

2:15 pm

Just back from lecture on body language = v interesting (as in I didn't visit land of nod, despite feeling like it).

Turns out that, if you fold your arms or cross your legs... you're an introvert, who isn't 'open' to other people and feels they have to protect/defend themselves in this way.

Got me thinking re how I come across, to other people like. Do I appear confident, or introvert? How does O see me?
Got me thinking also about how I look, like my face/hair/body – whole package.
OK, so O says he fancies me loads, but is he just saying that, coz that's what you're supposed to say when in a rel, innit? Does he actually find me... hot
or not?
Hmm.

The whole 'being super-SC&O to impress O' still has potential, and not intending to drop it or anything, but wonder if a bit of an overhaul in looks dept would also help... help keep him keen, and confident that I'm THE ONE? Thing is Bob, he's only human, and a bloke-human at that, and blokes like to look at serious totty... am I right or am I right? Also

Sorry, had to cut you off there... had most amazing phone call eva!

1st, this polite-sounding lady congratulated me on... winning a holiday (for 2)! She said something re a questionnaire I'd filled in somewhere, re something, and how they were all entered into a draw or whatever...
Unreal!
Where?
Abroad?
Wow – will need to:

1] *Sort figure (to fit correctly into bikini, which don't currently own, but am now toying with idea - not every day one wins a holiday after all!).*
2] *Book bikini line appointment with whoever does Lib's... not had it done before tho, but must be worth it.*

Am SO excited!
This might be just what me and O need, to cement our newly-discovered love... to relive the passion we 1st let loose in Romania, but under more

romantic, plush conditions... hurrah!

Lovely phone lady said I needed to come to some kind of presentation day thing, to claim the holiday... wow – is this how lottery winners feel, huh?! Think she said can bring O too – fab!

Sorry, back to business... yeah, ought to tackle my state of aesthetically-challenged-ness... make bit more effort, like sort un-obedient hair out, remove eyebrow stubble on more frequent basis etc.
These geeky glasses don't help – time for contacts?
Losing a stone or 2 would also help... maybe is time to start easing off on calories (good job cashews have nil calories, eh?!).

2:54 pm Yes, Bob – I know they don't REALLY have nil calories... am just trying to perk my sad self up a bit... that alright with you, huh?!

Fri 6 May

2:57 pm

Crack open the champagne (code word for 'cashews')... Jude has started her revision!

No, now am being unfair on myself... HAVE revised previously to today, but not for more than ½ hour, and not really convinced was absorbing info from text book in v effective way (E *Enders* v good this week – makes it impossible to concentrate).

But today, my E *Enders*-less revision has lasted for... 2 hours 10 mins!
Have just finshed. Feeling v proud of me, so thought would tell you – the best listener, I know (with my O coming a close 2nd tho).

The reason for my outburst of real work (apart from exams starting nxt week)? Well, when got in from Fusion last night (well, this am), was more knackered than usual – made swift decision (whilst fixing my hungry self an after-work snack of bowl of C Nut C Flakes) that I CAN'T go on working at Fusion, AND do this degree, AND spend quality time with my new bloke, AND prepare for my free holiday!

Rang Libs in bit of a panic. Bawled eyes out as soon as she answered, as all tired/washed-out/emotional etc... and coz had just spilt C Nut C Flakes all over lap (v messy). She was a star – seemed to understand... told me not to stop work altogether tho (she knows I can't afford to anyway). Said she'd rearrange the rota so I can drop Mons and stick to just Weds and

Thurs (I'm talking like she OWN's the club or something, when she only actually arranges the rota, but she's allowed to do what she likes with it, as far as I can tell!).

Thus, now feel happy that will be working less, and now feel ready, willing and able to throw my keen self into my study and

Oooh – phone!

Was Abby, inviting me over for meal before work. Said yes (like, I HAVE no other response to offer of free food, esp Abby's!). So, am off there now; ttfn, my cutie.

8:13 pm Just told O (via text) re Libs altering rota – he's well-chuffed… said he's been thinking I work too many hours anyway!

So – Abby's… well, weather not bad so we took kids out for walk (which is silly expression when related to Eve, seeing as she just lay in pram the whole time – no 'walking' involved whatsoever!). Nat did lot of walking tho – his legs may be smaller than mine, but his enthusiasm for walking/talking/stomping on ants is way larger than mine.

At one stage he wanted to hold Mummy's hand, so I got to push the pram. Have decided there are 3 advantages to being official pram-pusher:

1] *You actually have something to DO with your arms/hands instead of folding arms in manner of 'watch out – hostile walker approaching' as per yesterday's lecture OR allowing arms to swing at sides, which, in my case, makes me feel and prob look like orangutang (correct spelling unknown, but you know what I mean – the large orange ape thing… oooohhh… just spotted how the spelling of the animal is connected with the colour of it – well, it does the way I spell it… I see what they did there… nice).*
2] *When going uphill, it is quite an effort, but this is good aid to weight loss – hurrah! Ought to borrow Eve more often (as long as she comes with pram and steep hill).*
3] *Makes me think what it would be like to BE a real mum, with own sprog etc. (Hmm… to tell O about feeling broody or not, that is the question!)*

Abby didn't seem to understand me wanting to lose weight (tho she's heard me go on about it so many trillions of times before she's prob sick of hearing it). Had gone there with clear intention of saying 'no' to pud, but ended up having 2 helpings (Mint Vienetta) and then finishing off Nat's as he didn't like it coz it was green. (Aren't kids supposed to love ice cream? Don't boys like green?). Won't happen again tho – must be strong-willed… must must MUST if am gonna look good for O – hope he'll appreciate all this one day, eh?

Sat 7 May

Arrghhhh… need more cash!

Just browsing thru girlie mag someone left in my room the other day… for £29.99 I could send off for some 'Penetrating Lip Augmentation Serum'. Don't laugh – it expands actual lip volume and contour by 40.7%, while increasing Collagen Synthesis more than 339% – it says so and, while I have NO idea what it means, something tells me my lips need it, but is out of my reach… bummer – how am supposed to alter looks without stacks of cash, huh?

Post-BURP Duncs did it on 'friendship' which was a bit ironic (good studenty word) seeing as he's Mr Lonesome at the mo, since his legendary split with Lauren. She was there, but did her best not to actually LOOK at him… you could feel the 'awkward' vibes in the air – bit grim really. Hope me and O never get like that.

Or should that be – 'O and I' never get like that? Whatever.
Grammar – who needs it!

Didn't really listen to content of Dunc's bit – some rant re the latest trend in the land of all things Cn, as is his way.

Oh, hang on tho… there was one thing I remember… he did say something re us all being aware that even friends can become 'idols' if we make them more important to us than God… esp boy/girlfriends… and he glared at ME as he said this bit!! Perhaps HE thinks that I think that HE idolises Lauren, or something. Odd.

Sun 8 May

2:42 pm

Just back from Mike's – our oh-so-fab uni chaplain (a few of us went there for lunch, post-church).

Today's sermon was hilarious! Well, not actual sermon, but the way in which he (the minister) did the links between the various points he was making. Was rather like 'Comedy Dave's tedious links' on Radio 1 (on Moyle's show… not sure if they do these on show any more, as not listened to it much recently, what with having new b/f, life etc). Let me give you a couple of examples:

'Yes, surfing. I really did enjoy my weekend away, watching other people surfing – what energy they had! And you know, when you consider the lack of waves there actually were, it can make you think of dodos, in the sense that there truly is a lack of them...

...and dodos are, or were, birds... birds that roamed the land, because they couldn't fly...

...and something else that can't fly, my friends, are cars (unless you consider Chitty Chitty Bang Bang, which I'd rather you didn't, just for this morning)...

...and cars, cars go fast, because they have engines, but they also break down...

...and something else that begins with the same initials as break down, is Bàd Day...

...so, the question remains. Are YOU having a bad day today? Huh? Because, if you are, you'll know how Jonah felt when he was in the whale... and speaking of over-sized man-eating fish...'

Am I the only one who finds this sort of thing so majorly rib-ticklin' to the Nth degree? (Whatever that means.)

Didn't share all this with O, as would rather spoil my super-SC&O attempt... but me and Sas had a good girlie giggle over it.

Must be off and revise now... 1st exam on Tue... that's like 2 day's time man!

Mon 9 May

9:34 am

Just got up... 2 main objectives for today:

1] *Book app with opticians – suss out if can have contacts or not (price etc).*
2] R E V I S E

For some reason the 'men' in charge of our exams have arranged 2 exams, 1 day after the other (this week), then a week off, then 3 exams within almost 24 hours, then another 5 days off and the last exam – now, wouldn't it be better to spread them out a bit? Baahhhh! (Said with large hint of disgust.)

11:42 pm Ahhhh! (Said with large hint of gooey loveness.) Have enjoyed a v romantic eve with O – we went for a massive walk in some woods somewhere – tree stumps came in v useful... I stand on them while we kiss (me being such a shorty and all). He surprised me by asking me to come with him to visit his dad… in prison… tomorrow!

Says he'll pick me up from exam and we'll head straight there!

Sort of chuffed that he wants me to meet him, but sort of freaked at same time… not been to a prison before. Talk about adding stress to the whole 'meeting your b/f's parents' thing!

Will go with him tho – kind of curious, I guess, tho didn't say that to O, as didn't sound v respectful of, erm, the imprisoned.

Must pluck eyebrows… don't want his dad to think his son's going out with a lass who has uncontrollable eyebrow stubble (which, sadly, is quite true).

Tue 10 May

Post-*Friends* (series 2, I believe)

Prison visit report: O drove us – took about an hour. Thought we were stopping off at services, but turned out we were driving into the prison grounds, just like that – with no armed security guards, large bolted gates, barbed wire… nowt. Turned out this place where O's dad has been placed for the last few months of his sentence is an 'open' prison for 'lesser' offenders. From what I could see, the prisoners could do sport, had Internet access… could even study for degrees – wild!

And O's dad himself? A convict, a madman, a 'rouge', a ruf n ready inmate…

He was none of these! He was so 'normal' it was spooky. A normal, well-presented, interesting, polite, decent man/dad/potential father-in-law (?).

After an awkward few mins, the convo got going a bit – he asked me all about myself – my course, my friends, my hobbies (eating, TV – pref at same time) etc. Might have gone on a bit too long – O cut me off just as I was starting on what I thought about the appalling lack of decent loos on campus, and what I was hoping the pres of the SU was going to do about it (an important issue, but guess O kinda wanted to chat with him too, seeing as we only had an hour).

They caught up – he sees him at least once a week, so was all quite trival on the 'news' front, but could tell they needed to talk – are lot closer than I realised.

At one point, we got onto the subject of Maisie (his mum, O's gran, my enemy-turned-friend… now deceased). He said how much he missed her –

more than he imagined he would, esp as he couldn't be with family much. Regretted choosing not to go to her funeral – said it seemed best to stay away, at the time,

'For your mother's sake.'

O just looked down and started scraping minute amounts of dry mud from bottom of one of his trainers. It all went quiet for what felt like an eternity, and then some, but Pete (his dad's name) broke the silence with,

'People talk about low fat, high fibre cooking these days... more like low taste, high risk with my mum!'

and we all had hysterics.

He also said he hoped Radox (her cat) had a good home now, saying how much Maisie worshipped that manky moggy. O went rather pale, and looked as tho he was about to swap attention to the other trainer... but then he admitted he had no idea about Radox's whereabouts, and would look into it.

When we left, I almost couldn't understand why he had to stay there, and couldn't come away with us – *why* did he have to be there? Had he really done something to deserve it? Certainly didn't LOOK like a criminal, or behave like one.

Said this to O on journey back – he said that, if I'd lived through what alcohol turned his dad into at home, and what he put him and his mum thru (esp his mum), then I'd understand. Point taken.

Post-Robbie Hmm – seems like Robbie too knows what alcohol can do to people (ie him). Book says he's t-total, as is his only way to cope now. Pete is too – is that only coz he can't get alc in prison? O is, coz of what he's seen it do to others, he says. Makes sense. WHY does alcohol seem like such a 'cool' thing to consume/brag about/puke up, when it is, in fact, a complete nightmare? Huh?

Hang on... 'rouge'? Isn't that another name for blusher?

Scalp zits

Sat 14 May

I am normal.

No, really – I am. Jude Singleton is normal. (Stop that sniggering – it's the surname I was born with and will only be rid of when you, Bob, hurry up and marry me!)

How do I know this? Coz it says so on this chart here in front of me…

I weigh 60 kg (9½ stone) and am 1 m 56 cm tall… so I reside in the zone labelled 'normal' (tho admittedly, if I were one gram heavier, I'd be off in the land of 'overweight').

So how come I don't FEEL normal, but v v FAT, in style of Monica from *Friends* (when she was a teenager – DON'T tell me you haven't seen those 'flashback' episodes… they're sooooo wet-your-pants hilarious!)?

But feeling this fat isn't at all funny, and is almost made worse when pathetic (and most probably highly inaccurate) charts such as this one tell me I'm 'normal'. Wot crap!

Later Nothing much to report from this eve's BURP. No study – just an extended prayer thingy; I think with the purpose of praying for the world/starving millions/3rd-World debt, and all that… but found myself mainly praying that O will realise I'm just as 'all out' for God as he is, love me forever… and propose before we break up for the summer (but not out loud, for obvious reasons).

(Just to confirm – I meant that I didn't PRAY that last bit out loud, not that O can't propose to me out loud, which he'd have to – if he didn't, I wouldn't hear him… unless he did it by email/text… hmm.)

Ooooo – just remembered that something worthy of telling you did happen at BURP – a scrunched up piece of paper (A4, lined) was handed round, upon which was a few lines of scrawled writing, obviously done in a hurry, which read:

Dear BURP committee (and everyone else who goes),
Just to say, I'm sorry, but I won't be coming to BURP again, and resign from position

of Evangelism Secretary. It's just that I am really really busy with the band (called 'Nazarene' in case you'd forgotten – see website for details, and the opportunity to purchase our latest in-the-style-of-Coldplay-but-so-much-better album).

Hope to see you around.

Cheers

Reuben

There was a large stain covering part of the paper, which, if I'm not mistaken, could only have been made by a pint glass of Boddingtons, or sim.

Stunning – to think I actually worshipped the ground he walked on when I 1st met him! What a loser! Thought Fax would have a fit, being the boss and all, and being let down by one of the team… but he seemed chilled – said we'd just have to do without an EvSec and spread the work out to existing committee members. (Work – wot work? He didn't DO anything anyway!)

Ohhh… forgot to report back on this week's exams (Tue and Wed)… not too bad, but MUST make myself get down to serious revision asap, if going to survive the rest, which I am told will be harder. Annoying really – is not like they go toward final mark… just that I have to pass them to be allowed to keep going. How pants is that, huh?

Mon 16 May

Went to this 'prize draw holiday presentation' thing, with an unwilling O in tow. He seemed all suspicious, but assured him it was all kosher – the nice lady on the phone had said so after all.

A nice smart man welcomed us in to this posh conference-looking place – wondered if the local press might be there to take piccie: 'Student Wins Exotic Holiday' or sim. He led us into a vast room containing a sea of desks… full of other people! Huh?

The pattern went: 1 nice/smart person on 1 side of desk… 2 normal-looking people on the other; everyone deep in convo. We dutifully took our place on one side of the only vacant desk… and he on the other (got the feeling he'd done this at least a trillon times today already). Then…

OK, to cut huge story short (not my speciality)… the guy tried (hard) to sell us a timeshare apartment in southern Spain, and we, surprise surprise, were not interested. So the guy tried even harder and we were even less interested, and so it went – he just didn't seem to understand that students = no actual money = not able to buy TS apt, even if *were* remotely interested. Looking around, most of the others seemed as uninterested as we were, apart from at a couple of desks, where they were celebrating with champagne! The suckers! (O later pointed out that I was the real sucker, but I'll conveniently let that one go.)

And the holiday I'd won? Non-existent. Well, technically, I have won it, and am quite welcome to use it… providing I do so during certain specified time frame, in a certain way, and it could be to somewhere mingin' etc etc.

Life – wot's it all about, Bob? Not timeshare apts in southern Spain, THAT'S for sure.

During-'dramatic loss of free holiday' blues O just rang, all excited… said he had a plan. Got holiday on brain, so assumed he'd found us a great deal on 3 weeks in Jamaica or sim… but good job didn't open big gob, coz his plan was actually of a more important nature. He's gonna ask the prison chaplain about doing a sort of 'memorial' thing, at the prison, for Maisie. Told O I thought Pete would really appreciate that. He will. He's lucky to have O for a son. Blokes, in general, aren't known for being sensitive, but my bloke is. There's nothing 'general' about him, no sir-ee.

Fri 20 May

1:32 pm

Yuk! O's just left. Had great cosy eve together in front of TV, and even turned it off for 10 mins and had a pray (at MY suggestion – could tell he was impressed!). Had really itchy, bordering on painful, area on top of head, all eve. O eventually said he'd have a look.

'Ahhh – yes – I can definitely see what the problem is…'

The way he said that made me think he'd make a good doctor – I'd trust him with my life anyway, but in the next second I had minor panic – what could there possibly be to 'see' up there, but hair and dandruff… some kind of cancerous growth? A 3rd ear?

'A spot.'

Slight relief on my part, but then much wonderment – a zit, on my scalp… is that normal? Never had one there before… do other people get scalp-zits? Was it one of the few who so frequently 'hang out' on my face, that got bored and wandered off to pastures new… ON MY SCALP?!

BEFORE I had a chance to reply… POP! 'There – all sorted,' he said triumphantly, as in style of just having gaining a 1st class degree/achieving world peace etc.

Is this really acceptable – for newly acquired b/f to locate and eliminate my scalp-zits? (Arggghhh – saying that makes me realise I might have more of the little blighters!) A walk in the woods = acceptable. Watching TV = acceptable. Giving each other back massages = acceptable (tho not ventured into such territory yet), but this?! No no NO!

Still, perhaps I should be more positive, and view as a sign of our deepening rel – maybe this is what couples do when they get married – will ask Lydia tomorrow.

11:46 pm BTW, O said Radox is still 'at large' in the community! Seems like everyone thought that someone else was 'seeing' to Maisie's beloved cat and, in reality, she's lost and homeless (which doesn't bother me as not a big Radox fan).

Sat 21 May

Libs again backed off when I mentioned coming to BURP. Said it was,

'All very well for you Bible-bashing, happy-clappy Holy Joes, but about as much use to me right now as a BEEEP kilo of stilton.'

(She has such a way with words.)

Can't help but think that she needs BURP (well, God) more than ever right now – OK, so she appears to be hunky-dory on the outside, but what about all that abortion stuff, and the Prozac… surely she needs some help?

Got chatting to Fax about this, and he looked all serious for a minute, then said he was scrapping his study on 'Postmodernism' (planned for this eve) and that we were instead going to discuss 'BURP – the way forward' (shame, as always wanted to know what postmodernism is – must ask O).

After discussion in 2s, then 4s, then as a whole group (46, I counted), we had feedback (a term that always makes me feel hungry).

General consensus is that we need to concentrate more on evangelism, esp in the light of Reuben's departure (hmm… perhaps we could evangelise him back). With people like Libs on our 'fringe' (turns out a few of the others have friends who might also come), it has been decided to make BURP less like duplicating a church service (it couldn't be much MORE like one if it tried) and more of an outreach (but in cool, as opposed to cringe-city, way).

Saturday eves then will become our 'outreach/evangelism' time, and we will meet together for prayer/study/worship on a Mon eve. Ideas put forward for Sat eves were: open discussions on 'hot topics', silly games evenings (but '…not involving alcohol,' added Duncs, and I guess O was thinking this too) and a possible 'gig' of Cn band (pref not Nazarene – I added that!).

There were only a handful of dissenters… but O suggested they could be involved – just coz they weren't on the com didn't mean they couldn't help with the planning, blah blah butter-up blah. It worked – they agreed. He is a real peace-maker (as well as scalp-zit popper, but the less said re that the better). Drat – forgot to ask Lydia re that.

Just when I thought it was all getting a bit heavy (and not like the old days, when we didn't know quite what we were trying to achieve, but seemed happy with it anyway), Fax ended by saying he wanted us to go away from this evening with the following thought:

'Two wrongs may not equal a right, but three rights do equal a left.'

Those who didn't know him any better actually nodded their heads in agreement, but me and the guys just creased up, and it all seemed normal again – and Fax hadn't lost his powers of giving useless nonsensical facts at inappropriate times, bless 'im.

Tue 24 May

Just back from opticians – turns out I can get contacts for £13 per month (you get a brand new pair each month!) so am gonna go for this – bye bye geeky goggles… hello sexy contacts! (Not that contacts in themselves are sexy – I refer more to the fact that the LACK of goggles they permit could actually put me up one notch on the 'sexy' ladder, which will be useful as not even ON ladder yet, let alone v high up on it!) (Are you following me, Bob?)

Off to exam now… have actually revised quite a bit now – hope it pays off…

Post-exam Hard.

Hard.

And again… hard.

It was. The exam. The exam was hard. I found it hard. Hard, was what it was. Take back what I said a few days ago – now v relieved that exams don't count toward final grade… just hope I PASS, even if it's only just.

Sent O text when exam over, saying, without thinking, that I needed wine for my nerves, pref a whole bottle. He hasn't texted me back yet – is probably offended. How could I be so stupid? Telling someone whose life has been so affected by alcohol abuse that I'm gagging for a drink! Arrghhhhhh!

NOT part of my 'hold-on-tight-to-Oren' master plan.

Is not like I really NEED a drink anyway; it was more an expression really – to let him know how on edge I am re exams and all. Sure, I like wine – it would be nice to have some now… but I'd settle for diet coke (with vanilla) any day.

Hmm… what does this mean then? That I could live without alcohol? Could I? No. Unlikely. Perhaps if…

No. Esp when with others drinking in F&Ferret, like Libs… I'd look like such a wuss.

But if O can do it then…

No. That really would be taking the 'plan' a bit too far – would be too much like hard work…

Or would it?

You know, this might be just what's needed – only those all-out for God, the 100%-ers, super-SC&Os would even consider going t-total… yeah… OK, will tell O this eve.

Sorted.

Wed 25 May

Well, have managed to stay t-total all day so far…

The fact that it's only 9:52 am might have something to do with it, but why spoil things by telling you that, eh?

Big Brother started at the weekend, but I, for one, will NOT be watching it. Not because I don't like it, but coz I LOVE it far too much for my own good, methinks. If I watch this 1st one I'll only get totally addicted… buy *heat* for all the goss, cry when someone I've grown attached to gets evicted etc. Nope – it's a BB-free year for me.

BB isn't really something us t-total super-SC&O Cns are really into anyway – it's hardly the stuff of the God Channel after all, Cameron or no Cameron.

Right, off to work now… the staring happens a lot less now, and am more used to the job itself. Still, is hardly bundle of laughs, by any stretch of imagination.

Thur 26 May

V late

i am usin my lefdt hand torite ths to you cozl am usin rt handto holds down padz on

OK, am now unplugged from evil machine, and can type with both hands again. Was just getting ready for bed when Sas popped in with her new fab electrolysis machine, or so she boasted. Have been on at her quite a bit recently re my moustache – in the past have tried bleaching it, waxing (ouch city!) but it still grows back, just like my evil eyebrows do.

So, she said I ought to give this a go as it's 'permanent hair removal' and all.

It basically involved smearing stinky green gel on the area in question, then placing a white moustache-shaped pad on the area, and another circular white pad on my upper arm, with gel underneath (just in case you were wondering). There was this sort of overgrown pen-type thing (that wasn't a pen) that you plugged a wire into, then from that wire came a white wire and a green wire… the green one had to go into the moustache-shaped pad, and the white onto the circular one. Then you switched the 'pen' on, and the magic began!

Sat excitedly, dreaming of a life with no more moustache, a life of pure FREEDOM!

Was a bit awkward, as sometimes the connection dislodged, and the pen light would go off, signalling a lack of electricity 'flow'… so then you had to sort of prod the pads a bit, to get the flow back. But this messed up the timing, as a complete cycle consisted of 2 mins on, 1 min rest, then 2½ mins on again. Was all a bit hassly, and was reason why could only type with left hand, and right hand ended up attached to circular pad, to keep the flow… errrr… flowing.

At end of treatment, observed how v red my upper-lip area was. VERY red. Then read the small print – you have to do it every 2 weeks for up to a YEAR until you can guarantee the hair will no longer grow back!!

Arrghhhhhh! What a waste of time – no way am I going through THAT every 2 weeks, not even for Oren.

Still, at least glowing red upper-lip will be gone by tomorrow, won't it?

Fri 27 May

8:32 am

Hi Bob, and how are you today? If only I knew who you were, or more specifically – if I knew whether or not you were O. Am more and more convinced that you must be – how could anyone BUT O be the man of my dreams... the one God's had in mind for me all along etc etc? I wonder if

Nnnnnoooooooo! Just checked mirror – upper lip still looking as tho it's been in a fight and come off much much worse than the other guy/lip. Almost makes me want to cancel going to O's this eve, as is currently planned. Hmm.

12:77 am Just back from O's... had SUCH a good eve – despite suffering moustache (machine didn't actually manage to remove) and surrounding area.

Was just me, O and his housemates. Got watching CBeebies (on SKY)... at one point there were 6 of us crammed into the lounge, trying to keep up with the *Tweenies* singing 'Head, shoulders knees and toes', with actions. Sounds easy? Ha – well YOU try it when they tell you to not SING certain body parts, but still do the actions – not easy – even tho sober! Quite amusing that a group of the nation's so-called intellectuals have trouble keeping up with a bunch of colourful pre-schoolers (and their funky dog).

Mum would turn in her grave... not that she's dead... you know what I mean tho (I hope!).

Difficult to move much downstairs as Nazarene's drums dominate a large section of the kitchen, and some of lounge (O lets them practise there, much to the dismay of his housemates). Why he lets them do this, when Reuben isn't even coming to BURP any more, is beyond me... my bloke's just too nice for his own good (but it makes me love him all the more!).

Oh yeah – and here's another reason why this eve was super-de-dooper...

O bought me a pressie! No, not the engagement ring I've been dreaming about in spare time...

UNO!

As in, the card game, as in – the card game Rob Williams is obsessed with! He said I'd entertained him with snippets from Robbie's life for a good few weeks now, and he knew I'd been curious about the whole Uno thing – so he bought it for me – and is not even my b'day! How gorgeous of him!

Didn't actually get round to playing it.
Wonder if it'll become 'our game', like couples have 'our song' or 'our film'...
It could be the theme to our wedding – we could have packs of Uno on tables at the reception, in case people got bored.
No, swipe that... NO ONE will get bored at our wedding, it'll be the best 'do' since Posh n Becks tied the knot (but prob just a tad cheaper).

Quick correction It's not actually 12:77 am, as stated above, but is too late for me to be justifying this sort of typo, so will go now...

Tue 31 May

4:32 pm

V near v large lion! You're NOT gonna believe this, but I am, in fact, in London! To be more precise, am in Trafalgar Square, along with O, Sas, Fax and Duncs. Most of us have finished exams now – Duncs and I both had our last one yesterday, and last night he called a load of people and said, 'Hey – let's have a day-trip to London!' Most people were keen, but well-out of money. I am too, but O said he'd 'provide' for us both, which he v generously has done! Sas has money coz she now works (in Topshop, obviously) and Duncs has plenty of the stuff – geeks have a reputation for being frugal, I guess. Didn't want to ask Fax about £s, for fear of being bombarded with weird statistics I don't understand, and looking like dweeb in front of O.

Anyhow, we left v early this am (O drove) and got here around 9 am, and so far we've:

1] *Been on London Eye (V cool.)*
2] *Spent 2 hours in Harrods (Found a weird tacky 'memorial' thing, to Dodi and Diana, on some floor that we went to by mistake. In the centre were the actual wine*

glasses used by D&D, just before they left the hotel on the night they died, preserved exactly how they left them… which, in reality, meant they were MOULDY! Yuk! No disrespect to D&D, but when I die, I hope beyond all hope that I won't be remembered by the fungus that has grown from my well-old saliva or sim.)

3] Covent Garden (There were these people dressed as statues — looked like they'd been dropped in a large gold vat and then frozen for all eternity… and I was supposed to give them MONEY for looking this stupid?)

4] Been all over the place on underground. (My fave pastime ever!)

5] Nearly went to St James Park. (Until Fax pointed out that every year parks in London are doused in 1 million gallons of dog urine. Nuff said.)

Discovered that being in the capital is no different from being in Bymouth – on campus or in the town… blokes continually look at Sas as she walks by them (some gals do too – always a worry). OK, so she's hot… but why have I never had blokes leer at me like that? Shall I dye my hair blonde like hers? Bah!

So, here we are now in T Square… there's some sort of jazz thing going on – a great atmos. So many people. So many pigeons (or doves?). Wish I could come here more often – there's such a buzz of excitement, an odd sense of having 'arrived' – like all other places in this country are just poor imitations of this… the real thing.

Oh, in case you're wondering – am typing this on O's laptop (I have my own folder on it now!) which he decided to bring… who knows why.

Got to go now as need the loo. Rather tempted to travel back to Harrods. If heaven has loos, then hopefully God has had the sense to use Harrods' 'luxury washrooms' as the prototype.

Chubby bunny hell

Thur 2 June

1:42 am

OK, so who's hotter – Robbie or Justin?

This was main topic of convo at work this eve (yeah – they talk 'with' me now, rather than just 'about' me). I'm more a Robbie fan, I think, but I rather think I'm being influenced by his book (nearly finished it now) and so is hard to say. Justin's cool – tho not sure re his likeness to Michael Jackson (vocal likeness, that is).

2:10 am Ahhhh – just thought that you might not want to answer the question re hotness of male pop celebrities, being male yourself and all. Sorry!

Wish I could give you some of these cashew nuts to make up for it, but you're not here, so will have to finish the packet by myself – how tragic.

Sat 4 June

11:41 pm

Still haven't found Radox, darn it.

Bizarre/freaky evening. BURP was on 'marriage' (no, not as part of our outreach, we're not making 'the change' until this week coming). Fax had asked Abby n Amos to come and chat about how it is for them, and to answer questions etc. (I'd told him they were the best example of a happily married couple on the planet, which is probably true.)

Twas all going well – A&A were doing their stuff to the max, being all SC&O about it… I was just getting to the point of thinking partly this makes me feel sick as is too soppy, and partly am jealous, even tho am ½ way to being wed already (supposedly). Amos was saying something about communication – how it was 'the key to the success of any relationship', when LYDIA burst into tears and ran out!

Jon (her hubbie) just sat there, looking tres embarrassed – never seen him go so red. Amos had stopped mid-sentence, but Fax kinda nodded at him to continue, so he did.

Went out in search of Lydia after a couple of mins, hoping that O would realise how super-compassionate and caring I am… also that I'd get some low-down on what's going on (me and my big nosy nose).

We chatted, she shared everything with me – I ended up counselling/ praying for her well into the early hours…

…or, at least, that's what I would have LIKED to have happened!

In reality – couldn't find her, so made small-talk with a friendly vending machine, that ended up allowing me to have several items of serious snackage, for a small fee.

Hmm – wonder what it was all about tho – marriage probs? Seems unlikely – they've only been wed about 6 months… happily-marrieds don't have probs this early on, do they? Is that allowed?

Sun 5 June

Post-church

Still haven't got goss re Lydia and Jon – neither of them were at church, which has got to be a 1st. Tried to cross-examine Fax re it, but he just asked me to pray for them. Honestly – some people are just so anti-goss… am only being a concerned friend – couldn't he just have given me a teeny tad of info, like that they're:

1] *having probs,*
2] *splitting up,*
3] *under stress coz Lydia's preggie with quad-ru-plets (correct wordage?),*
4] *under stress coz Jon's preggie, and this really isn't acceptable practice for a bloke.*

Oh – did get some juicy goss at church tho… guess who's back together? The rulers of the Geek Kingdom… Duncs n Lauren!
Not really 'goss' as such – everyone could plainly see them all lovey-dovey-gooey-wooey…
Puke city, I say.

Am pleased for them tho – they've both been such huge pains in rear since the famous 'Spring Harvest Split'.

PS Some SERIOUS goss that's doing the rounds at the mo… PRINCE WILLIAM is visiting Bymouth Uni! Not sure when, but, hey – how cool is that? How hot is he? (Very, thx for asking.) If I could just get near enough to him to preach the gospel, get him saved... then he could be you, Bob! Sorted! No more budgeting! (Ssshhhhh... don't tell O tho!)

Mon 6 June

3:52 pm

Awhhh – O just did the cutest thing! I was complaining of tres runny nose, and was getting into a state coz had no tissues in room, and was almost crying re this (Time Of the Month – TOM)... and he popped out, only to return with...

some 'Winnie the Pooh' novelty tissues! Was soooooo sweet of him – made me cry (so not many tissues left now, only a couple of Tigger ones!).

He was mumbling something about them running out of normal ones ... but he's heard me talk about my Nan, and how she used to read me W the P stories all the time... he's so thoughtful!

God is so good, letting me 'have' a bloke such as O.

Tue 7 June

Collected contact lenses – they are SO freaky to put in and take out: takes me about 5 mins to do each task. If it always takes me this long, having contacts will take 10 mins off each day,
that's 70 mins off each week,
60 hours each year, which is 2.5 days...
which basically means that, if I live to be say 90, I will have spent 177.5 days (almost ½ a year) of my life faffing around with my darn contacts.
Smashin'.

Assume will get quicker in time (won't I?).
At least won't have to be a 4-eyes all the time, and will look hotter.

Is too hot at the mo (weather) – am too sweaty for words, so I won't include such words in this letter to you.

4:14 pm Am just watching something on ITV re 'education and our nation' or whatever. Has just occurred to me that perhaps my effort for self-improvement in looks dept ought to be extended to all-round self-improvement, things like general knowledge/politics/current affairs and the like. O knows ALL that kind of thing – actually seems to ENJOY the news (he thinks I don't know that he watches BBC News 24 in his spare time, when I'm not in his house, but I do!).

My IQ must be rated somewhere between 'could do better' and 'pure pants'. Perhaps O would like a more knowledgeable, interesting person to marry – someone who knows who's fighting who, and why, and can actually locate the relevant countries on a globe etc. Hmm.

8:19 pm Ha! Duncs just rang to say there's a pub quiz this Sun eve, and should we all go. Was just about to turn him down, when realised this could be my big chance! If I can swot up on… errrr… everything, before Sun eve… I might just get a chance to wow my man with my intellectual convo, and by helping my team to win the quiz – genius, c'est nes't pas! (Sorry, French never was my strong point.)

Wed 8 June

Hot hot hot and more hotness.
Someone direct me to the 'off' button asap – the sun has really been over-doing it these past few days.

Plan of action re pub quiz (which several of us are def going to, inc me and O!):

1] *Read newspapers (no Jude, not* heat… *real ones, like the* Guardian, *and suchlike).*
2] *Watch the news at every given opp (that's grown-up news and not* Newsround… *there is a difference).*
3] *Try to engage mates/work colleagues/friendly vending machines, in convo re world affairs… listen to their comments and ABSORB in style of massive 'gimme-facts-now' sponge.*

Bah – can't believe have got to work tonight, when could be watching *Newsnight* with Jeremy Paxman (words I never thought I'd hear myself say).

Thur 9 June

2:14 pm

Am waiting for O to pick me up – we're off on Radox hunt. Not really sure I WANT to hunt for that evil, demon-possessed (?) cat… but Pete's relying on us. O's fairly sure she's been taken in by a neighbour somewhere, and can't be too hard to locate. Hmm. Who'd take in Radox? Not me, coz

Ah, O at door – bye for now.

7:31 pm After a 4 hour intensive search, we've finally found: piddly-all.

We must've knocked on every door within a 2 mile radius of Maisie's house, but no-go. No manky moggy. O is gutted, and not sure how to tell his dad. I'm gutted for him, tho find it hard to muster up any sympathy for Radox (rather hope she's on other side of world, in a place where cat-meat is a delicacy).

O came back here for a bit, and was most surprised to discover copies of 5 different daily newspapers stuffed under my beanbag (quick note to self – don't use b bag as hiding place again) to save myself from having to explain, I suggested we pray for Radox/Pete, which we did (think I sounded convincing enuf, not sure tho).

Really freaky when O's phone went on the dot of our joint 'Amen'.
It was some posh bloke who's neighbour had told him about our search for Radox… and HE'S GOT HER!!
We're picking her up tomorrow – talk about answer to prayer!!

Fri 10 June

8:28 pm

Radox has been at O's house since we 'retrieved' her, but they're not really supposed to have pets in the house, so we need to get her housed, and fast. O's been ringing around all eve, but with no joy. I've even done my bit by ringing our pastor and getting something put in our church Sunday newsletter thing: 'Nice cat, needs good home – FREE!' (Please don't think I lied in the use of the word 'nice'. Just coz I don't think she's nice, someone else might… I think.) (Not.)

Pete would have her like a shot if he was… well, if he wasn't… you know, in prison.

Sat 11 June

Post-1st BURP outreach thing

Ah. Not good. In fact, disastrous. Duncs and Lauren did a sort of 'silly games' thing – chubby bunnies, and the like. Hmm… that game always makes me self-conscious – imagine people are lookin in my direction thinking, 'Wow – there's a serious chubby bunny.'

Poor turnout – about 15 (mainly the committee, a few faithfuls… and I think all of 2 genuine 'outsiders', who both left before the end… well, after the 1st 10 mins of chubby-bunny hell). Think D&L were rather too caught up in their own scary world of oh-how-wonderful-it-is-to-be-back-together to realise how dire it all was, and that playing Amy Grant's latest hits (of the 80s) on continuous loop in backround really did NOTHING to help.

Oh – hang on – 3 outsiders… Libs was there too. She seemed to find whole embarrassing experience highly amusing. She won c bunnies – 14 marshmallows, or thereabouts. Typical. Fax cheered her on – does he fancy her? Are they an 'item'? Naaaa – couldn't be. Fax wouldn't go out with a non-Cn, would he? As BURP president, would he get the sack if he went out with her? Who would sack him anyway, he's the boss?! (Apart from God, I guess – what would HE think?)

Lydia & Jon there, but not sitting v close together… things look a bit strained.

Sudden thought – all these couples breaking up, getting back together, having probs etc is all v unsettling – makes me question the stability of my rel with O. How do I KNOW it'll last forever? Where's the guarantee? Would it help if I just got on and proposed asap?

Sun 12 June

3:57 pm

Church OK. No response to my classy cat ad tho.

Pub quiz this eve. Have watched so much TV news, read so many papers, and subtly asked clever people (but not O) so many questions since Duncs' phone call… what I don't know re the world we live in, just isn't worth knowing!

11:46 pm Just back from quiz. At some pub down road from F&Ferret (our local) but can't recall name of it.

Competitors: Me & O, Duncs & Lauren, Mike & Jane, Fax and Sas (Libs would've come but covering someone's shift at Fusion, as she so often does). Mike was buying the 1st round (he's one cool chaplain!) and, without thinking, I asked for ½ pt Dry B... had to dash up to him at the bar to change it to a Diet Coke, after O gave me a 'Oh-so-you're-not-sticking-with-the-t-total-thing-then' look. Shame really – alcohol could only have improved my performance this eve (in the sense that it would be impossible to have made it any worse).

I was crap. Even after all that swotting. None of what I 'absorbed' came up in the quiz – only a load of stuff I hadn't a clue about. Got it sussed after a bit tho... the trick to looking (almost) as intelligent as your fellow teammates goes as follows:

1] *As soon as a question is asked, raise both hands to mouth, whilst at the same time causing your body to go into 'upright' mode, and saying in slightly raised voice:*
'Oh... oh... it's... it's... Hang on, I know this... It's... oh... oh...'
(You won't feel silly – this is what most of the others will be doing anyway.)
2] *Continue in this fashion, with v strained look on your face, as if you're searching every possible section of your memory for this 'temporarily misplaced' information.*
3] *Wait until someone in your group actually says the right answer (it'll be the one when several others suddenly start nodding/mumbling in agreement) and then adopt a relieved look, sigh, then say:*
'Ahh – that's it/I knew it/it was on the tip of my tongue' etc.

Sorted.

This kept me going for most of it – even O was fooled (I think).

Guess general knowledge is more of a 'lifestyle' – not something you can learn overnight.
Well, I say 'pants' to general knowledge/pub quizzes/Trivial Pursuit and the like... which just goes to show how uneducated and common I really am. What is the likelihood of me ever getting to be Mrs Oren if I don't know the capital of Shri Lanka (correct spelling?) (question no 17, part b). Huh?

Mon 13 June

10:35 am

Just got distress call from Sas. She needs someone to go to school and 'do puppets' for Year 1. She's doing BEd and is on her 'placement' at Bymouth Primary... and is increasingly becoming the most stressed individual on the planet. SO glad I didn't opt for teaching degree.

Saying that, what exactly AM I gonna do with Psychology degree? It all sounded so appealing and cool a year or so ago – but am beginning to wonder about wisdom of my choice, esp when they give us such pants lecturers.

So, have agreed to help Sas out. The school are having an 'Arts Week' – Sas had booked her mate (who's doing Performing Arts) to visit class she's working in, and do puppet show. He dropped out early this am, and now she's in major panic re it all – doesn't really look good for her if she fails to produce the promised puppet show, I guess. Tried to tell her that:

1] *Puppets aren't really my thing,*
2] *Kids aren't really my thing (sure, love my niece and nephew tons, but kids that aren't actual blood relations... naa).*

But so desperate was she that she wasn't in any way interested in my protests... rather think she'd contacted a whole load of other people before me, ones who actually have some smidgen of 'puppet' ability. Huh.

So, O's giving me a lift down there in ½ hour (she's already there). Is all good 'life' experience, I guess...

Post-puppet 'life experience' I never want to see another kid from Year 1, or Year 'anything' for that matter, ever, ever, EVER again. Was exhausting!

Actual puppet thing went OK – Sas had all the 'gear' ready and organised (such is the nature of trainee teachers) – all I had to do was to pop my hands into a couple of puppets, and read my lines (*Goldilocks and the Three Bears*).

I thought I was dire. Sas just got on with it, clearly v aware that everything she did might be judged by the 'real' teacher (who was sat at desk behind kids). In all honesty, real teacher appeared to have giant mound of paperwork to do; hardly looked up at our show... was prob just glad to have someone else to amuse her class for a bit!

And the kids? They LOVED it! You should've heard them literally scream with laughter! Thing is that, with this age group (errr, 5-year-olds, I think), the expression 'wet-your-pants-laughter' can become more than just an expression, if you catch my drift! Still, not my problem, thank goodness (REALLY put off even considering doing PGCE now!).

Sas had planned to get the puppets to sing some nursery rhymes at the end, so the kids could join in. We did 'Humpty Dumpty', but then both had complete mental block re what to sing next. Kids were getting restless, and teacher was starting to look more at us than at her pile of books... so I just went for it with the 1st song that came to mind:

'A Pizza Hut
A Pizza Hut
Kentucky Fried Chicken, and
A Pizza Hut...'

The kids all knew it (bizarre!) and sang along with great gusto, for ages... even after we'd finished and were packing up, and they were supposed to be moving onto 'clay play' or whatever. Can still hear their little high-pitched voices singing it in my head (1st sign of madness – hearing voices?).

OK, so the kids weren't all that bad (and didn't once question why G Locks and co were singing about fast food outlets), but wouldn't opt to do it again in a hurry. Sas really owes me one.

Quite late Radox update: text from O has just informed me that Mike & Jane have agreed to house Radox! Cat-lovers, apparently. Just wait till they meet manky old Radox tho – enuf to put anyone off the feline species for life!

Tue 14 June

9:41 am

Just had phone call from Abby – checking I'd remembered about helping at Nat's 3rd b'day party today.

Kinda went AAARRRGGHHH down phone (so loving sis would be aware I'd forgotten, and take pity). I'd SO forgotten about it – she'd asked me to help, like, WEEKS ago (and, unlike her, I don't have diary/calendar that tells me exactly what am doing, when, with whom, why, how etc).

Told her re yesterday, and how it was really exhausting working with all the KIDS and I could never work with KIDS… she took the hint – said she actually had a lot of 'Mums' that were staying to help – didn't really need me anyway. Cool. Hate to let her down, but really would be kiddie-overload to be exposed to 10 'Nats' this am: Pass the Parcel, Musical Statues etc – far too much like hard work.

Still, hope they save me large slice of cake (bound to be Bob the Builder – Nat's his biggest fan)!

Must get hair cut – my split ends now have split ends = not good.

Wed 15 June

11:04 am

O and I popped over to give Nat his pressie. (Abby said he'd have so many pressies etc yesterday that it'd be nice for him to have another one today, when all has calmed down!)

Was so much looking forward to seeing his little face light up as he opened his Bob the Builder duvet cover and pillow case set!

No light radiated from face, just tears… lots…

'Bop a Bill-der? … I wike PIDE-ER-MAN!'

He stormed off to play with his newly-acquired pressies from yesterday, mainly Spider-man-related ones.

Huh! Like when did HE grow out of one kiddie-character and move on to another, without informing his fave (only) Aunt? Abby says he 'made the change' about a month ago – she could have told ME! Kids these days… there's no commitment… not like in my day… what's wrong with B the B anyway – looks like fun to me, and I'm 19!?

Ungrateful nephew came round in the end (after O had little chat with him). O suggested we take duvet cover set back to Argos and swap for Spider-man one, which clearly our best (only) option. So perked up was Nat that he started singing:

'A Pizza Hut,
A Pizza Hut'
And so on.

Abby looked at me, rolled her eyes – complained that they'd all been singing that for most of duration of party yesterday... apparently some of Nat's older friends, who're already at school, had picked it up from somewhere.

Hmm. No prizes for the Bob who can tell me what school THEY go to!

Legged it out of there before she discovered the inflicter of the most annoying song in history on her household was her own 'skin n blister' (apologies if you're not a Londoner and don't speak the lingo) (not that I am, but Nan was, and teased us with such phrases often).

12:30 pm WARNING: BOB – PLEASE DO NOT READ ON if you are in any way squeamish, don't have an affinity avec small insects, or are just about to eat your tea or whatever...

The grimmest thing EVER has happened to me. Well, has been found ON me. Well, in my hair! No – not scalp zits – we've been there, done that and bought the T-shirt already... this is FAR worse.

Think 'alive'.
Think 'crawling around'.
Think 'NITS'!!!

Was just hanging out in Libs room, busy discussing the pros and cons of those big flatten-your-tummy-knickers, when, with no prior warning, she leans over me, peers into my hair, and says, 'Hey babe, you've got lots of little friends living in your hair – how quaint.' I ran back here asap, to have extra-extra long, hot, shower. During which it gradually dawned on me that nits can't actually be washed out. Arrgghhh!

P A N I C, P A N I C, P A N I C!!!

Guess I got them off Nat – kids always have nits/worms and the like, don't they? He's the kid I see most often... can't believe Abby has allowed him to:

1| *Get nits,*
2| GIVE THEM TO ME!

Am gonna ring her now and sort her out...

Errr, right. Seems that Nat has not got (nor has ever had) nits. Abby got me to think about what other kids I'd been in contact with... and suddenly dawned on me that must have got them off a member of Bymouth Primary's Year 1 puppet-loving class. Whoops!

Still, locating source of nits all v well and good, but does not help me rid head of them… am scratching head continually – is prob more the thought of them than the actual blighters, but still… is real nightmare.

HATE the thought of them creepy-crawling around my head. Yuk city.

Abby turns out to be the source of all wisdom re nits (says she is preparing herself for when her kids DO one day get them – remind me not to have kids, or at least not to have kids with any hair on head). Here's a gem of info she passed on to me: the itching is due to the fact that they are sucking blood out of my head! Like, hey nitty dudes… I've only got 8 pints (only know this as was answer to question 7 at pub quiz) so go steady!

Also, it's not the bug things that are called nits, it's the eggs that they lay. Great. Not content with doing their 'Buffy' act on me, they're also playing happy families. Can just hear them now:

'Let's see who can lay the most eggs and have the most Buffy-babies on Jude's head – on your marks, get set… LAY!'

Am NOT gonna tell O – this really is too embarrassing for words – is not like I invited the Buffys on board or anything, but can't help thinking this must mean my hair is manky if it attracts such creatures.

I have an appointment with the nit-exterminator (aka Abby) this eve at 9 pm. Begged her to sort me out NOW, but she was way too busy with kids and making meal etc.

So here I sit, alone… unless you include my cling-on Buffys.

Infested. Being drained of my own life-supporting blood. Providing a suitable home, and environment in which Buffys can raise their kids. Trif.

Just looked on Internet – typed 'nits' into Google, and now really wished I hadn't. Get this – they don't need hair/heads to live on, oh no: they can also live in carpets and UNDER your FINGERNAILS!

On reading this, grabbed nearest pair of scissors and hacked all nails as short as poss. No way they're getting under there too. How do I know if they're living in my carpet? How foul – feel like ripping it all up and burning it… but guess uni wouldn't be too impressed with such a gesture.

One useful site (American) said to use tea-tree oil on head, as they don't like it. Very thought of being able to inflict THEM with something THEY don't like is highly appealing, so off to buy some T T oil now – think all T T stuff is currently on offer in Body Shop anyway…

Post-B Shop Popped into Topshop to see Sas on way back, as it occurred to me that SHE might get nits off the kids, and ought to know about them asap.

Turns out she's had them loads already, and knows all about them. (How come everyone is a nit-expert all of a sudden, huh? Did I miss the nit-awareness training day or something?) She's now coming round at 7 pm with her 'gear'. Interesting.

O just rang – did I want to go round to Mike & Jane's this eve to babysit Jack, so they can have an eve out together? Told him I didn't, so he asked why: I just bluffed my way through it, saying I was tired/studying/still suffering with hayfever etc. He seemed a bit 'off' with me after this, and kept asking if 'everything was OK', but I assured him it was (no WAY he's gonna know about the Buffys).

Post-Sas On entering my room, she commented (loudly) that I STANK. Which was fair point as I do, due to T T oil, whole bottle of which is currently on my head. Have sort of got used to smell now (either that or it's damaged my nostrils so can no longer smell). Seems to have relieved my hayfever too!

Sas brought along her trusty 'electronic nit comb' thing – it let out the most excruciating of high-pitched squeals – got her to stop after a bit, in case it killed ME, which really would defeat the object of the exercise.

Was just off to Abby's, when she rang and said she was so so sorry but couldn't 'do' me this eve after all – but I can go over tomorrow am.

Right, am ringing Fusion to say am 'sick' and can't work this eve. Think having nits prob qualifies as being 'sick' – I'm certainly not 'well', am I?

12:35 am How exactly am I supposed to sleep, knowing that the Buffy-lice are aboard, huh? I've tried everything – cashew nuts, Hollyoaks, study (not for more than 10 mins tho, obviously), ringing mates... nothing is taking my mind off it.

2:31 am Still awake. Are THEY awake – do they ever sleep, or just feed/lay eggs all round the clock?

2:46 am Am never going near a child again. Will keep at least 5 metres away from anyone under age of, say, 10. Sorted.

How to enforce tho? Hmm.

A severe lack of Big Brother

Thur 16 June

All done! My darling devoted sis spent a good hour wading thru my infested hair… squishing anything that crawled. She got rather too much pleasure from the squishing part, if her little Dr-Evil-style cries of 'Mmmwwhhooaahahaha… gottcha!' were anything to go by.

And she calls herself a pacifist!

Still, bad news is, she says this needs to be done each night for next 2 WEEKS! This is how long it takes for eggs to hatch out, apparently. How does Sas cope with all this? Anyone doing a BEd/PGCE ought to be given an allowance to hire a nit-exterminator, who'll 'do the biz' each eve for 2 weeks, imo (that's short for 'in my opinion', altho I've just spent loads of space explaining what it means, so it's not 'short' for anything now…).

Can't afford bus fare to Abby's every eve, what to do?
Tell O?
Risk him dumping me for someone who can guarantee him a buffy-free zone?
Not likely.

Fri 17 June

Thought for the day (but less profound than those on Radio 2).

Is it more 'Cn' to ignore what we look like – body image etc – because we're all made in God's image, and all beautiful, whatever shape or size. Or, is it more 'Cn' to keep our bodies 'trim' because this means we're looking after the bodies God has given us?

Alright, you sussed me… this is really to do with being fat or slim, as always. Where do you draw the line between being 'healthy' and watching your waistline because of this (and being obsessed by diets etc and forever on scales, then having a good cry, then eating 2 slices of sticky toffee cheesecake and a Solero for breakie) (like I did just now)? Hmm.

O says he likes me the way (size) I am. So, would he DISLIKE me if I lost weight? What about if I put ON 3 stone?

Think will stick with 'healthy eating' type idea – it will sound acceptable to O, and yet will help me lose weight, which I really must do, b/f or no b/f.

Sat 18 June

Instead of another (disastrous) BURP outreach eve, we had a mtg to discuss how best to 'go forward' with them… we all tried not to criticise the last one too heavily, but again, don't think Duncs & Lauren would have cared, or even noticed, if we did, so 'in love' were they. Sometimes they make me feel inferior, as if O and I should be like that – 'close', 24/7. We are close tho, just not so 'in yer face' about it, when in presence of others. Saying that, he's a bit weird with me at the mo – has been since I turned down that babysitting the other eve.

To 'win him back', I told him all re nits (well, someone's got to de-nit me every night, and can't see Libs or Sas volunteering to do it). He was narked I hadn't told him straightaway – said I shouldn't keep stuff from him. He even asked if I was keeping anything ELSE from him! Ha – as if!

After mtg (at which nowt was achieved, as far as I could tell) we all headed to F&Ferret… I was on the diet Fanta – you'd think O would appreciate my efforts to keep off the booze, but he seemed more concerned about us 'sharing' and 'being real' with each other, or something like that.

Lydia was saying something about a low-sugar jam that she liked, which I took an interest in, as part of my new 'let's get healthy/slim' plan. (Jon not at BURP or pub.)

Fax rounded the jam convo off by saying that during WW2 some women were employed to rub minute pieces of wood into seed shapes so they could be added to raspberry jam, so it could be made without the aid of actual raspberries!!

Kind of puts you off jam.

PS How does Fax KNOW these things? Must find out what he's doing degree in – have never thought to ask. Perhaps is new BA in 'Useless facts', but what job will that get him… vicar?

Sun 19 June

Church was useful – learnt that Jon & Lydia now having counselling from Mike & Jane. Wonder if it's about sex – Jon wants it all the time and Lydia can't hack the pace, or Lydia wants him to wear…
OK, nuff said.

If it's true that whatever you eat just before you exercise, you burn off during the exercise (or something like that)… and if it's also true that whatever you eat AFTER exercise won't have too much effect on you as you're still burning off fat, or whatever, sounds like a v good case for eating Pringles before and after a lengthy jogging session round Bymouth. Will have to give this some thought.

Mon 20 June

Everyone on about 'housing' now, for Sept. Sas is sorting me and her out – she's still so grateful for me helping out with puppet thing (which I remind her about at least 4 times a day).

She'd die if she were too far away from her retail therapy (mainly clothes), so can guarantee will be living nr town centre next year – hopefully it won't cost me too much tho. Also, she can use her feminine charms (the tart) on any male landlord… wish I had a powerful weapon such as this.

Think about driving every now and then… in the sense that I'm not doing it, even tho passed test few months ago! Why? Coz:

1| *I don't have car,*
2| *The v thought of actually driving in a car without dual controls (and someone who can use them if nec) totally gives me the willies.*

Still, one day… perhaps.

Tue 28 June

Whoops! Bit of a gap – sorry!
Nowt of any interest to report from last week really…
Work at Fusion quite good – almost enjoy it now!
O still being a bit odd with me, but he'll prob be back to normal soon.
Only 2 more days of having to be checked for Buffys! (O doing fab job!)

Not watching Big Brother is pants. Can't go ANYWHERE without overhearing people talking about it...

'Yeah – but I wouldn't want to sit NEXT to someone who farts that much... let alone LIVE with them... it's unethical!'

or

'Oh no – I disagree... have you SEEN the size of her boobs? He's GOT to fancy her...'

and so on. It's like real life is passing people by, unnoticed, while everyone saturates themselves in the 'fake' life of the BB household. I speak from experience – but one that I've learnt from... Never again will I be drawn into the evil time-wasting clutches of BB! I've got a degree to study for and a b/f to see after all!

11:26 pm Keep sitting down to write this entry to you, but end up in floods of tears, head resting on desk in front of keyboard... mind blank... but also full

full of

hate confusion depression desperation self-loathing fear numbness

Make no apologies for being morbid – is just how I feel right now.

O has dumped me.

OK – typing that set me off again – even had Mr NextDoor round, saying he'd heard me crying and wanted to check I was OK (how he heard me over his M Manson album is beyond me, the freak). No, sorry – he's not a freak, he's actually a v decent bloke, oddly enuf, proving that appearances count for v little (in sense that he looks spookily like his fave singer... well, actually he looks plain spooky full stop).

Right, well, thing is... me and O are no longer together.

Came completely out of the blue. I was over at his place, in his room – we were in middle of discussion re BURP and the recent changes etc, when he suddenly blurts out:

'...and Jude, I don't really think this is working. I mean 'us', we're not really... working, are we?'

I sat in silence as he said quite a LOT of stuff about feeling 'distant' from me... like I wasn't being myself when we were together – how I always seemed more relaxed when I was with other friends...
and other such stuff...

Brain kind of froze over, assume with sheer shock of it all. A couple of mins, later I moved into depression mode, when I realised that this fab bloke that was saying stuff to me, had been MY fab bloke, up till this exact moment… and now he was DUMPING me. A few mins after that (told you he said a lot), I drifted into hate/anger mode…

How DARE he accuse me of this crap!

Now I'm here, alone, just flitting between all modes known to man (and woman). 'Fear' crops up now and then… fear of being alone for rest of my life… will I ever find a bloke that likes me? Will I ever get over O? Will I feel like this (tres tres crap) for eternity?

Is it me? Am I so ugly/boring/unintelligent/unspiritual that he can't be bothered with me any more? It's not like I didn't TRY – surely I get 15 out of 10 for effort – doesn't that count for something? Huh?

Wed 29 June

Cried myself to sleep last night. Am not after sympathy, Bob (well, guess I am really), but is SO hard. So hard. Harder than anything have ever come across before.

Woke up this am, sort of felt OK, but had definite feeling I'd been depressed the night before… and promptly burst into tears, yet again, when I remembered why.

So, am yet again a singleton.

Jude Singleton – singleton by name, singleton by nature. Is somehow worse than before when had never actually HAD a bloke, but just wanted one badly. Now I know what it's like to have one, and have actually been careless enuf as to lose him… is more pants than ever.

And do I want a bloke now, you ask? No, I want O.

By which I mean that, I know O IS a bloke (in case you had any doubts) but I think I want him, and only him. I think. Do I? Yes. WHY? Dunno. Just do. A lot.

Is a stupid chick-flick type phase, but is on my mind anyway:

'Where did I go wrong?'

HOW could I have blown this?

WHY did God set this all up for me, if he knew I'd mess it up?

DID God set it up for me, or was it all huge, huge mistake?

IS all this kind of talk just evidence that I am obsessed with O, and am giving him more time and energy than I'm giving God?

No, sure answer to last question is 'no'... everyone feels like this when they break-up, right?

Would pray about it, but guess am kind of cross with God too.

Oh – called in sick at work again... just can't face doing anything right now, let alone work. Lucky for me that Libs is in charge of rota, otherwise would prob be getting a warning re pulling 2 sickies recently.

Fri 1 July

Day 3

My life is governed by the fact that am no longer with O.

No longer a 'pair'.

A g/f.

One ½ of a couple.

One ½ of 'we'.

Skipped work on Thur eve, meaning have had 2 work-free days, and not intending to go out today, which puts me into Day 3 of this unbelievable hell called 'break-up'.

4:32 pm Sas just called in for a bit (told you gossip spread fast here). She went on about how depressed/stressed SHE was, re the workload the BEd is putting on her. Not sure exactly how that was supposed to help ME. Guess it took my mind off O for a bit (only a bit, mind) as was consumed with willing her to SHUT UP about it and let ME have a turn at getting sympathy.

Just as she was going out the door (and being ogled by Mr NextDoor, who appeared in the corridor just as my door opened – what a coincidence... not... the perv), she took my hand in hers, and said how hard it was when Reuben dumped her (a few months ago) but how she's over it/him now.

Felt like saying 'AND...?? Your point being...??' or 'Oh – well that's all hunky-dory then, innit? I'll just wait a few months and then I'll be just fine... why did no one tell me this before... thx SO much for enlightening me!'

But just forced a smile instead, and closed the door, fast, leaving her in corridor, and huge chubby grin on Mr NextDoor's face.

What exactly am I supposed to do in these 'few months' anyway? Lock myself in my room? Book a place in the nearest nunnery (where nuns live – correct spellage?) till I'm 'over him'?

How do I know I WILL get over him anyway?

Is he thinking any of this, or is it just me?

Is it always easier for the 'dumper' as opposed to the 'dump-ee'?

Probably.

Sat 2 July

Day 4 BURP

We are postponing the 'outreach' Sat eve things till next term, when we might actually come up with some decent ideas that actually work. Just met for prayer and chat this eve. Fax told everyone how much he was looking forward to what I had in store for them next Sat, and did I want to give flyers/posters out, so everyone could help with promotion?

'Huh?' thought I.

Then it hit me… A few months ago I'd agreed to sort a special event for end of term… one we could invite 'outsiders' to, a kind of fun thing, but with the intent of outreach etc. Just when you think you're getting away with leaving outreach till the safety of after the summer… you're reminded that you're expected to put on something BIG and DECENT… in a week's time!

Why did no one mention this recently? Did they think I'd actually REMEMBER to organise it? OK, so I'm SocSec and all, but no one ever said that THIS kind of thing was part of the deal.

Guess is partly coz Reuben, evangelism secretary, abandoned us… got ½ a mind to track him down and make HIM do it.

The guys at BURP didn't realise how lucky they were I was actually THERE, seeing as I've become such a master of skive recently… and then they expected me to announce details of next week!

Just told them it was a surprise, and that I'd get flyers etc to them all asap. Nightmare.

This is just the kind of thing O would sort out for me, if we were still together.

He wasn't at BURP… quite relieved really – not sure I could face him right now.

Sun 3 July

Day 5

How long will it be before I stop viewing life in terms of how long I've been apart from O for?

Dragged myself to church (in hope that sermon might have subliminal message:

'You will get back with Oren... he made a mistake... don't worry.'

Or, better still...

'You are still with Oren... this is all a dream... pinch yourself real hard on your right butt-cheek and wake up.'

He was there.

V v awkward – didn't know whether to say hi or not, to sit near him or not, etc. Looked as tho he didn't know either... so ended up with neither of us going anywhere near each other. He looked normal. Guess I'd rather hoped he'd look as tho he'd been thru what I've been thru, and have a tear-stained face and all... but guess I looked normal too, so hard to tell.

Duncs n Lauren took pity on me and sat either side of me, making me feel like the cheese and marmite in a geek sarnie (they both consume scary amounts of such sarnies... must be a geek thing). They tried desperately to get out of me who I'd got coming to the 'event' on Sat. (Didn't even know I was expected to get someone else to do it... what's wrong with me... aren't I good enuf?)

Lauren said she was hoping for a Cn celebrity, such as:

1| *Nicky Gumbel*
2| *Matt Redman/Tim Hughes*
3| *The Tribe*

But Duncs pointed out that I was unlikely to have been able to get A-list Cn celebrities. (Why not – don't they think I have connections? I don't, obviously, but they don't KNOW that, do they?) He reckons we'd be more likely to get the guy who makes the coffee for the band who 'supports' The Tribe... or the girl who is the sister of the bloke who 'drives' for Steve Chalke (he backed this up by saying he knows Steve Chalke HAS a driver coz he saw the job advertised a few years ago!).

Hmm...

Who to get...

in under a week?

Wish I felt even slightly motivated to really go for this event thing… but don't.
Can't imagine feeling motivated to do anything ever again.
Life has lost meaning.
I have lost O.
I am lost.

Mon 4 July

BURP was WILD (in a good way!). Something I hadn't imagined myself, or any self-respecting human being, ever saying again!

Inspired by the pub quiz the other eve, Fax did one for us!
But no stupid questions re capitals of countries I can't even spell etc… just a ton of stuff based around Cn-ity, and the like.
Well, it was last BURP of the year… if you can't let your holy hair down then, when can you let it down, huh?!

(That reminds me – must get hair cut asap… situation is past 'pressing', and rapidly moving in direction of flippin' desperate.)

O not there – no one knew why.
Almost forgot about O for a bit, till we were leaving, and saw Fax chatting with some BURPers, wishing them a fab summer etc.

Reminded me just how fab O is at that sort of thing. He's such an ace person to be with at a party… just chats to everyone and anyone… not like he's all extrovert or anything… just manages to find common ground with great ease and speed, has plenty of self-confidence… so unlike me. I tend to avoid like pubonic plague (correct? Sounds like a puberty-related plague, that can't be right, cannit?) anyone who's not on my course, or at BURP, or at church, etc. But O… he's a genuine social being.

I love him.
I miss him.
Lots.
Bbbaaarrgghhhhhh!!!!!

Tue 5 July

Weird day. Seriously weird.

Pauline was just about to say something REALLY interesting (for a change)... when Libs rang and asked me to come to her room. Obediently gathered together the snackage items I'd got lined up for the eve (2 mini-tiramisus, cashews and 5 remaining triangles of giant Toblerone) – figured I could watch the rest of E *nders* in Libs' room, and toddled off... (well, toddled 'up' – her room on floor above mine).

After opening the door for me, she slumped onto her (unmade) bed... looking about as down as I've ever seen her. The room stank of fags... even the open window was doing little to help... made it real nippy too. She only had her desk light on... so was kinda dark. Hoped she didn't expect me to stay for long... TV wasn't even ON!

Stood there for a sec or 2, wondering where to put my precious snackage, without it getting too contaminated with fag smoke, etc (room was right tip). Then she whispered:

'Look at this babe.'

Sat upright, slowly took her T-shirt off.
No bra.
Hmm.

OK, so she's always a gal to surprise you... and has a habit of doing what you'd least expect... but showing me her boobs? Huh?
Has she turned lezzie?

Didn't know what to say, but soon realised I was totally gawping. Had good reason tho – further study of boob-age revealed they had orange felt-tip drawn on them – several circles worth.
A new craze of boob-art?
Some kind of sex game gone wrong? (Almost wished had read Oscar's sex books, so could offer appropriate advice).

She just sat there, looking at me, looking at her decorated boobs.
Bizarre.
What does one SAY in such situations?
Fortunately, she did the talking.
Not the jokey up-beat stuff she usually comes out with... just an account of what had happened, followed by some serious crying.

In a nutshell, she'd decided to have a boob-job, then backed out.

(Altho in habit of ripping up any cheques from lottery-rich parents, she'd always fancied bigger boobs, so a while back just asked them for £3,500 – just like that... and they gave it to her... just like that!)

Literally minutes before she was due to be put to sleep, she chickened out – said the whole 'doctor-in-white-coat' thing took her back to THAT day... the day she let her baby die (her words).

After pulling her T-shirt back on, she'd beckoned me over... I ran. Dropped snacks – they went everywhere. Did I care? Nope. Some things are more important, and this was one of them. We hugged and sobbed for stupid length of time... at least an hour, I reckon. Like she said tho, how do you know when you've cried enuf? When does it end? Does she even WANT it to end? If a day comes when she doesn't feel like crying about it, isn't that as big a tragedy as what she actually did?

Have no idea of answers. Didn't seem like good time for crappy Cn God-can-fix-it-for-you answers. Still, I offered to pray with her, and she nodded, so I did. Hard to get words out tho, when you're crying so much... so so much. Didn't finish the prayer... so we just sat there, grasping each other's hands like our lives depended on it... saying 'amen, amen, amen, amen...' like it was some magic phrase that would do something... anything... to help relieve the pain.

After pouring herself a large shot of vodka (a triple?) and adding a mere 'dash' of coke (full-fat)... she said that when I'd prayed, she'd suddenly thought again about how I'd been on at her to have counselling. That Fax had been on about it too... and that perhaps now was the time she ought to go for it,

'To prevent me from turning into total Prozac junkie, like.'

Will ask Mike about her best options re counselling asap.
Am SO pleased she's made this decision.

So, yeah – weird day.

Wed 6 July

Hair cut = not good. Too short. Yeah – I am aware that purpose of a hair cut is to make hair shorter, but in my case I SPECIFICALLY asked her to get rid of split ends, while *keeping* the length... is only in past month or so has got long enuf to put in tiny plaits, Geri Haliwell-style, which look real cool, imo. But NOW I find it's too short to do this… BAH!

She must've taken a good 5 cm off.

Sorry – am getting so hacked off with almost everything… is due to depression, induced by O, so blame HIM.

S'pose the split ends might have gone that far up… wouldn't surprise me.

Fruity farts

Thur 7 July

'Ere's a thought. Just coz am no longer with O, does this nec mean I chuck all my 'improving myself' efforts in nearest skip? If we're NOT getting back together (which is looking increasingly poss) then isn't that even MORE reason for me to make myself more... interesting? To know more? To look better?

Sooooo don't feel like I'm back on the shelf now... v thought of 'being' with a bloke other than O just freaks me out bogtime... BUT, what about the 'I've started so I'll finish' thing, huh?

Sorry – that typo meant 'bigtime' became 'bogtime', but have left in, as:

1] *it's quite amusing, and I need all the laughs I can get,*
2] *it's actually quite a useful typo – has reminded me I need a pee real bad, must dash.*

Ahhhhh – sweet relief!

With this on mind ('improving myself', not 'bogtime') last night I got chatting with a lass at Fusion. She's doing BEng, and SHE knows LOADS of stuff! She was raving on and on re *Ulycees*, by Joyce someone-or-other... seemed to think it was best novel in the world, ever!

Went straight to uni library this am and got it out!

Am looking at it now – alarm bells are ringing... it calls itself 'A Reader's edition'. Like, why do we need an explanation, or help, to read a novel... It's in english, innit?

Oh, is by JAMES Joyce, it seems (not Joyce, which is a relief, as would really seem wrong for world's greatest novel to be written by someone called Joyce).

OK, now I've actually opened the book.

Hmm... think will skip the 83-page 'introduction', that has intention of making novel easier to read, but looks as tho will confuse me all the more. Will just read the thing...

Yeah, right... Not really 'getting into' part one. What the Jeeves is he going on about?

Will move swiftly onto part 2…

Fascinating… if you're into the details of a bloke that's constipated and what he gets up to on the loo, which I'm not. Grim. Just this bloke going on and on and on re himself and stuff – how bor-or-or-ing. He get's all his tenses muddled up too – and I thought this was supposed to be a classic! How it ever got past the publisher I'll never know!

OK, now find myself on p647…

where there are 88 pages with no full stops or commas whatsoever imagine that how can he do that its so bizarre I dont think it would go down v well if I handed an assignment in like this but guess authors can get away with this sort of experimental stuff making one massive sentence last 88 whole pages he mustve been real bored oh changing the subject slightly I forgot to say that bumped into Reuben on way back from library and couldnt think of much to say so told him of my dilemma re this Sat eve as in the outreach event thing he said I ought to do a Celebrity Big Brother type thing but a Cn version of it that could be called Celebrity Big Brother in the Lord CBBITL for short and I could get all the top Cn bods to lock themselves in a student house somewhere and have them vote each other out throughout the day and then get the winner to do the final meeting in the eve hmm wasnt quite sure if he was kidding or not esp as he proceeded to think about who might be in it and who would fight with who and so on bless im the weirdo is not like hes really one of us anymore so is not in position to give advice really CBBITL honestly well really dont think this one massive sentence thing is my bag baby is it yes no didnt think so and am I gonna take this beastly book back to library this very day yes I said yes I will yes.

Fri 8 July

9:31 am

Ahhh… bliss, just had ½ hour with latest *heat* mag… now that's REAL writing for you!

C lens update – are getting quicker to put in and take out, but find em real itchy, bordering on painful when tired, which, being a student, is a state I am contracted to be in until I graduate.

Is it still worth me paying for C lenses now O can no longer appreciate them (or lack of goggles that they allow?). Yeah, probably. Kind of like them anyway. Got to get O off brain, but how? Still so down re whole thing.

AND still not sure what am going to do tomorrow eve… asked Mike 2 days ago if he knew anyone who could come and 'do' something. He said he'd get back to me… but hasn't yet. Nightmare.

10:04 am Just been down to get post – letter from Pete:

Hi Jude

I can't tell you how pleased I am that Oren's found someone as lovely as you! Thx also for your help in tracking down Radox. I'm so relieved she's finally been housed, and Mum (Maisie), if she's looking down on us all, will be pleased too. I look forward to seeing you and Oren on Tuesday, for Mum's memorial service.

Regards

Pete

Wow – how nice is that! To say I'm 'lovely'!

So O hasn't told him we're 'apart' yet then. Hmm. Had totally forgotton re memorial thingy. O will have to go alone. Shame, had been keen on the idea, and wanted to support Pete. Maisie was special to me too, after all (in a crazy, cranky old-lady type way!).

Mike got back to me this eve – no, he doesn't know of anyone who can come and do event tomorrow. Great. Fab. Will just have to chuck whole thing in. Unless I do it myself?

Ladies n Gentlemen, please put your hands together for…
JUDITH SINGLETON… the great entertainer-cum-evangelist…
I think not.

Will leave till the morning, then fake illness, or do whatever I have to to get out of this stupid thing that I am incapable of doing without divine intervention… arrhhhh… makes me realise have not really prayed re it… so will now…

Sat 9 July

8:31 am

Fax has just rung – he's been back home for couple of days, and only just found out there's been NO publicity re this eve's event… and WHAT ON EARTH WAS I PLAYING AT???!!!

I KNOW, I should've told him the truth, but felt so so so guilty, and he really wasn't the calm cool person he normally is… think I got scared really – told him it was all 'in hand' and I'd ring him back later today with details. He started to ask how on EARTH we were going to publicise an event that is supposed to be happening in 10 hours time…

I hung up on him. Not something I make a habit of doing, but it seemed my best option at the time.

Options? Huh! My only option right now is to top myself (might have to jump from Libs' window tho – mine isn't high enuf to cause any serious damage… previous experience tells me) and leave a note in jeans pocket:

Dear BURPers

I am so so sorry that I failed to get anything sorted for this eve. Can't tell you how bad I feel re whole thing. I totally forgot about it, then just couldn't get head round organising it as so depressed re the fact Oren has DUMPED me.
Hope you understand.
Yours morbidly,
(The late) Jude

Can't see any other way to avoid getting chucked off committee. Hate it when I mess up. Really don't need this right now, esp as… ah, phone… hang on a sec…

Was Libs – told her all… she went all quiet, then said she had an idea, and would get back to me in an hour.

Huh? Wot idea? Wot Cn speakers could SHE possibly know?!

Just used some of my hour-of-agonising-waiting to ring Abby… turns out it's her n Amos' wedding anniv today! Had no idea. She said no worries tho – wouldn't expect me to remember, which made me feel even MORE guilty (I was their bridesmaid after all).
SIX YEARS they've been married – that's, like, AGES!
Am trying to stay focused on being happy for them, and not wander into 'jealousy' territory again, as so oft happens.
Still – 6 years… bless 'em.

Right, if Libs is anything like the pal she claims to be, she'll ring in exactly 3 mins, and… ahh.. phone!

Just off out – meeting Libs at library to run off some posters/flyers:

HRH Prince William… talks about his year out in Chile.
The White Hall, 7 pm, THIS EVENING (Sat 9 July)
SEE YOU there!
Bymouth Uni Revival Plan (event organisers)

Turns out that P Will is visiting our uni this very weekend, and HAD been expecting to do a talk for the uni 'Chile Association' this eve. Was some kind of mix-up tho, as it soon transpired (this am) that Chile Association folded last month, due to lack of membership (surprise surprise). Libs happens to know the pres of Students' Union, and that this particular lass had been flapping around all morning, trying to organise P Will's tour of uni, whilst stressing re disappearance of Chile Association.

SO, Libs just told her that BURP would have him instead… and would organise entire thing! She was more than willing.

I AM IN CHARGE OF AN EVENT THIS EVENING, TO WHICH THE ENTIRE UNI IS BEING INVITED…
AND PRINCE WILLIAM IS THE SPEAKER!!!!!!!!!!!!!!!!!!!!!!!!!!!!!!

No time to get head round whole thing… am v important SocSec to v important uni organisation… must organise organise organise (or at least help LIBS organise!).

6 pm Hmm… is all going to plan. The White Hall is just about the largest venue on campus – has seating capacity of 500! Libs says this is necessary, as we'll have ½ the uni wanting to come… personally, I'd be happy if we got even 100 people (including us BURPers), but think it might feel a bit 'empty' if we're left with 100s of empty seats. Still, she seems to know wot she's doing.

Publicity has gone well – had most of committee frantically handing out flyers/putting up posters, all day. Is just a matter of waiting now… Am going to The White Hall at ½ past, to meet SU pres, Libs, Fax… AND THE PRINCE!!!

Have to admit am feeling rather wet-my-pants style nervous… if I'd known I'd be meeting P Will a few months ago, could've done crash diet, sorted hair out, had face lift, etc (c'mon – he's well hot, AND loaded).
All reminds me of how Robbie W says he feels just before a gig… all nervous and empty.
This eve MUST be a success… won't need to top myself if it isn't – Fax will probably do the deed for me!

Post-BURP Summer outreach event Ha! It was Fab Fab Fab!
So much to tell you!

Was bit freaked when 1st got to The White Hall, as O was there, chatting away with none other than HRH. Sort of assumed he was avoiding me (O, not HRH) and wouldn't make an appearance this eve. How wrong could I have been! He kind of compèred the thing, and did the 'interview' with P Will, after he'd done his talk (with slides! Only a prince could get away with showing slides to students and not looking like geek king!).

Will's talk was good tho – OK, so turns out he was only in Chile for 10 weeks, not a whole year, and it was a good few years ago that he went… but still – he said how it affected him, made him think re the world and how we treat it and how privileged we are in this country etc.
O then asked him some really deep (but interesting) questions… the crowd was hooked (crowd = 500 odd, plus the ones who stood!).

Whole thing only took an hour. O finished by saying a bit about how he related to what Will had said, coz of his time in Romania etc. He challenged us all to rethink our attitudes to those less fortunate than ourselves… to use our education to educate others, even mentioned that God created us all and how it must really nark him that we are so busy with looking out for ourselves that we don't bother about the rest of the world etc… AND, get this…
right at the v end he asked everyone to bow their heads, for a moment of prayer.

½ expected people to start making dash for the doors, but instead, 500+ students dutifully bowed their heads, while O thanked God for what Will had achieved and experienced in Chile, and asked that we would all be able to fully comprehend how we can play OUR part in helping the people of the world… the people HE made and loves etc.

After the throng had parroted his 'Amen' (a moving moment if ever there was one), he said we ought to all show our appreciation to P Will for sharing with us his…
…but before he got any more words out, the clapping/cheering began… the bloke even got a standing innovation! (Correct wordage? Perhaps it's 'ovation', but that sounds more like something relating to my TOM!)

Duncs & Lauren then swang into action, organising willing BURPers to hand out doughnuts n beer (chilled)… for free! Even Reuben was part of their team… funny how EX-committee members come out of the woodwork when royalty comes to town… don't blame him tho!

Sas, Mike and Fax were doing a bit of 'follow-up' work, handing out tracts to anyone consuming free edibles, or with evidence of having done so (face covered with jam/sugar, and poss a bit tipsy).

Tracts? Yeah, but not your normal cringe-city ones... some cool ones that Fax had designed a while back and he'd altered slightly to suit this eve's event... explaining what God etc is all about, giving info re uni chaplain (Mike), BURP, local churches etc. Never seen our little unimportant, low-profile committee work so hard... I just stood there, exhausted, wondering if had all actually happened, or if was in middle of crazy dream!

I also helped Libs 'liaise' (good word) with the local press, who were everywhere.

Made me laugh to see so many people with doughnut/beer in one hand, and phone in the other...

'...no, Mum REALLY – I'm not kidding – he's right over there – I can actually SEE HIM from where I'm standing – yeah – how cool is THAT?!'

Prob ought to contact the *Guinness Book of Records* re – 'The Uni CU outreach event that attracted the largest audience ever ever!'

Had just bitten into 3rd doughnut, when a light tap on left shoulder made me turn around to face tapper... twas P Will!

He was well nice – thanked me for organising it all, said it went v well etc. Wanted to say that actually Libs had been rather... errrr... instrumental in organising things... but is impossible to swallow large mouthful of doughnut that fast, even in presence of royalty (also, didn't want to spoil illusion of me being the events organiser of the decade... perhaps he'd have a job for me back at the palace?!). So just nodded and smiled a 'doughnut-wide' smile, before he was whisked away by some tall bloke (bodyguard?).

Didn't see O at all – he must've left real early. He was so good – really connected with P Will; totally got respect from his captive audience. You'd think he'd be a bundle of nerves, but was as cool as a crispy, crunchy cool cucumber. (Why do people say 'cool as a cucumber? Surely there are other refrigeratorable items that are a good deal cooler, like cheese... why don't we say 'as cool as stilton' eh?)

Reuben walked me back – he was narked coz P Will didn't seem too interested in his convo re Nazarene, and the future he has in mind for them etc. Like, what was he expecting – a promise of a gig at Buckingham Palace?

Wow – that was a whole lot of doughnuts/beer we gave out... guess Libs must've found a good use for her boob-job dosh after all!

If I was back with O, this would be one of the v best days in my life so far.

Sun 10 July

Skipped church, as v knackered (and quite frankly, overwhelmed!) re last night.

Finished Robbie book instead...
Almost thought he might be potential Cn for a min, when read that he prays before each performance... till turned page and turns out he prays... to Elvis!
Does that count? Prob not.

Really must play Rob's fave game (Uno) again – played it so much when O 1st gave it to me, but haven't touched it since we broke up.

'Broke up' – such a graphic phase... Is just how I feel tho – broken.
In need of mending.
Separated.
Hurt.

Mon 11 July

4:31 pm

Was so down today that spent all day so far reading psych text book. (Yes, that's how bad it is...). Discovered section on 'break-up of relationships'. Some survey they did showed that the partner who was 'less committed' in a relationship tended to take advantage of any natural 'break' points in the year, to end it. For example (it said)... students might finish with their partner AT THE END OF TERM!!

Trif – so this proves it... O was the 'less committed' in our little pair, and simply can't be bothered to continue the rel into the Summer hols. Well, that's that crystal-flippin'-clear then. Huh.

Sort of helps that people I don't even KNOW are coming up to me and saying how much they enjoyed the 'P Will' thing... but only 'sort of'.

Had spam email thing today (one I actually read) that waffled on about eating only fruit for a week to lose weight. YOU were supposed to order their book to help you with it, but all looks like plain sailing to me, so am going for it.

Roll on slim, fruit-loving Jude. Fruit is nice, anyway, so shouldn't be a prob. Will go to Tesco now to stock up…

Post-Tesco Just had 2 apples, ½ yellow melon and a banana… yum! How healthy am I?!

Tue 12 July

8:24 am

Breakie: 1 bite of kiwi fruit (chucked the rest as yuckier than had imagined), 1 orange, 1 apple, bowl of raisins… so far, so fruit-i-ly good!

12:42 pm Lunch: 1 banana, other ½ of yellow melon, 2 pears, millions of grapes (well, it WAS a large bunch!).

Am feeling too bloated for words.

Am farting like the biggest grimmest farting monster ever imaginable.

OK, so fibre is important… but it's clearly poss to go OTT.

What if I bumped into O, then farted one of these stinky, fruity farts in his presence?

Nope – am giving up… would rather be fat than farty.

3:32 pm O IS ON HIS WAY OVER HERE TO PICK ME UP!! He just rang, to 'check' I was still coming to Maisie's memorial thing, at the prison. Huh!

Couldn't BELIEVE he'd think I was still intending to go, seeing as we're not together anymore… but he clearly had other ideas… Said Pete was expecting me, and it'd be a bit thin on the ground without me etc. Notice he didn't say anything about HIM wanting me there, but is prob coz he DOESN'T, but is just looking out for his dad. Ggggggrrrrrrrr!!

Said I'd go in the end – would feel too awkward backing out at this late stage, seeing as I'm 'expected' to go.

Nightmare.

6:41 pm Back again. It wasn't too bad. Prison Chaplain did a good job. Moi got all emotional over Maisie again – still find it hard that she died so suddenly, and I didn't get to say goodbye etc. Crying for her (which I did during the service, much to my embarrassment) only nudged me into thinking re my own Nan's death… which set me off even more. Felt O's arm round me just before the service ended. Went all hot n cold at same time. Only one thought whizzed thru my teeny brain – I WANT HIM BACK.

But it wasn't O's arm anyway – on opening my eyes I realised it belonged to Pete (they had been standing either side of me).

Pete seemed to appreciate our efforts – he cried too, but said he felt like he'd actually said goodbye now, and was more 'at peace', so that's cool.

O hardly said a word to me in car or whilst we were at prison… but then I hardly said a word to him either – guess we're both feeling real awkward re whole thing.

How I wish that had been *his* arm.
I want his arm.
I want *all* of him.

Wed 13 July

Weak and frail as I am, I have given in to a force higher than myself – indeed, higher than all of us. Of what am I speaking?
Big Brother.

May it be known that, 7 weeks into the show, Jude has succumbed to the lure of BB, and will be watching it every night from now till the end. Good job not going round to O's, or would watch it 24/7 on SKY (would love to go round to O's tho, if he'd have me back).

(Gonna video this eve's or will miss it due to work. How sad am I?
Don't answer that.)

Libs grabbed me in a quiet moment at work (we have v few quiet moments… it is a club after all). She's got her counselling thing all sorted – had her 1st visit today. Asked her if she got any good advice. She just laughed, and said that counselling was more about listening than advising.

Huh – how was I supposed to know?
Wonder if someone would listen to me waffle on re losing O?

Oh, on that subject… Sas has gone and got herself a bloke!

Some bloke who's just finishing his BEd, and has survived it (she says he's inspired her to keep going with it, and she's less stressed re whole thing now). He's not at BURP, but have seen him at church before – nice bum, funny shaped head tho. Hmm.

How can she bag a bloke as easy as pie (a non-fruit pie that is – I am avoiding all fruit now, even references to it in these letters!)? OK, so she's totally hot, but WHY WHY WHY… when I can't even keep the only bloke

I've ever been out with?!

Bet she won't even put any effort into the rel, like I did with mine... prob just 'be herself' or whatever. Bah!

Mind you, she couldn't really improve her looks if she tried... and is already well gifted (she was so good with those kids at school – she'll make a great teacher), and me? I'll make a great, fat loser, at this rate.

PS Is there such thing as a non-fruit pie? Hmm. Unsure of answer, and too tired to search brain for 'pie filling' section.

Thur 14 July

Ha – joy of joys... Sas has sorted our house for Sept!
3 floors
6 bedrooms
2 bathrooms
is nr to town-centre/campus... not cheap, but a reasonable deal, all things considered... according to my personal house-finder!

Residents: Me, Sas, Fax, Duncs and 2 other BURPers, more Duncs' friends than mine, but they seem OK. It was thought (by the likes of S&V flave Duncs) that Cn couples are not wise to live in same house, due to the temptation that this would put in their way. Thus, Lauren is living elsewhere.

Sas' new bloke (wannabe teacher, nice bum) already shares a house with some other ex-students. Wonder if O would've moved into same house as me in Sept, if we were still together... would Duncs, the ultimate VIRGIN on campus have allowed it? Would it have been good for us, or damaging to our rel?

Why do I even bother with such irrelevant questions?

1:34 am WELL-embarrassing thing happened at work. Not in the usual 'Jude-smashes-yet-another-glass' sense tho... bit more subtle than that, but still made me feel real pants all the same.

Basically, I was yapping with the others at end of our shift, re the new girl. She started last week – doesn't say much. I was just saying something about her looking a bit like Marge Simpson, and sounding like Homer (she often says, 'D'oh!'), when Libs interrupted me, and told us all to get a move on and clear up so she could lock up. When the others had obediently dispersed, she gave me a right talking to – how dare I gossip about someone I hardly know and haven't made an effort to talk to. Didn't I remember how I felt when I 1st came and the others stared all the time and talked behind my back? And (worst bit coming up)…

'… and you call yourself a Christian, Jude… get a life, chick!'

The v worst thing is that she is soooooooo right! I was really enjoying my 'laying into the new girl' bit – even made people laugh (not a regular pastime of mine). But I DID hate it when it happened to me… How can I BE so unthoughtful/insensitive…

Libs really seems to be thinking about God n stuff these days. Pity she isn't in my house next year (she's living with mates from our course). Will really miss her. Still, will be nice to be in house-full of Cns!!!

Right – am going to watch this eve's BB now… just about managed to learn names of all residents now… is more a matter of latching on to the group's dynamics, sort out who fancies who… etc.

Fri 15 July

Yip yip skippie-de-do-dar… going home tomorrow!

Is not that I am in any way excited re prospect of being at home with boring parents in boring town for entire summer… more that I've had ENUF of this place, and need to get away. Away from lectures and study… but mainly away from O. Somewhere inside, I think I have decided that to be distanced from him by many many miles, will help me to acknowledge that we are well and truly over, and there's nowt I can do about it. At least I'll get a bit of peace and quiet – is not like parents will play M Manson till 4 am or anything, unlike others I could mention (namely Mr NextDoor).

Ooohhh – that reminds me – must pop and say goodbye to him… He will NOT be sharing a house with me in Sept (thank the Lord). Will do it now…

Aaaaahhh! He really is a sweet guy… he said he'd miss living next door to me, and that he was so used to hearing my cute snoring at night that he doesn't know if he'll be able to get to sleep without it in Sept (I don't snore… he was obviously kidding!).

4:32 pm Just had a McDs with Sas (not avec her new bloke tho, which was relief, as not v good with 'couples' right now). She asked me to tell her exactly what happened when me and O broke up.

Went thru entire thing, bit by bit...

1] He said 'I don't really think this is working out.'
2] He then said loads of stuff about feeling 'distant' from me, and how I wasn't myself when we were together.
3] We broke up.

Not satisfied with my account of events, she wanted to know EXACTLY what he said during [2]. I said I hadn't a clue, as brain went into shock, froze over etc.

Tried to focus real hard tho, while consuming McChicken sarnie (which clearly helped) and came up with:

'I think he said things about me "trying too hard" to be his g/f, and that's why he couldn't relate to me properly...'

At which point, Sas leapt in with a rather scary 'Ah-ha!' and proceeded to ask a string of awkward (and downright nosy) questions... the result of which has revealed the following:

1] I DID try too hard to be his g/f... went about it all the wrong way.
2] I DID try to be someone I wasn't, which can't have been easy for O.
3] I AM a total idiot – breaking up was MY fault, and not his.

She said I had to go and talk to him, face to face. I have no choice... I'm off to his place now... Wish me (Cn) luck!

Post-O visit Result? None, as I got all of ½ way up his road, then chickened out like huge cluckiest chick-chick this side of McChickensville. Grrrr... Why am I such a wimp? All I need to do is apologise for being so... so... CRAP, and ask for a 2nd chance.

Right, will try again – might even make it to his front door this time!

Post-2nd O visit Result? None. Oh yeah – I made it to his front door, even knocked on it, even had it answered... but he wasn't in... He's GONE HOME. Went 2 days ago, apparently.

NO NO NO NO NO NO NO NO NO NO NO NO NO NO NO NO NO NO NO!!!!!!

Sas says that this is the kind of thing that can't be done via post/phone/email – it has to be face to face. What to do?

Sat 16 July

Called in at Mike and Jane's to say my farewells… Jack (their little 'un) was all cute and cuddly – will miss him! He led me to the conservatory, and pointed to a gorgeous cat, all curled up on a whicker chair, sleeping in the sunshine. Its fur was all shiny – looked like they'd got themselves a smart pedigree cat from somewhere (can you get pedigree cats, or is that just dogs?). Under pressure from Jack, I went over and stroked it… it woke up and stretched, displaying it's full glory. Not really a cat-lover, but couldn't help thinking this was one flash moggy!

Jane walked in and said 'Ahhhh – you've been re-acquainted with Radox then?'
No. It couldn't POSS be, thought I…
Talk about a clean-up job!
They even had flea charts up on kitchen noticeboard… how many years it'll take to move her army of fleas out I can't imagine (still, as an ex-nit-infested person, I can hardly talk!).

WHY I am bothering to talk about my ex-boyfriend's deceased-Gran's transformed cat… is anyone's guess.
S'pose she makes me think of O.
Like Libs suggested, I really should GET A LIFE.

Timmy Mallet rules OK

Sun 17 July

Is weird, but nice, to wake up in old bed, in old room, in old house... etc.

Journey back with Dad yesterday went OK. He's not much of a talker (no one who lives with Mum for long is allowed to be much of a talker). The few things he did say were enquiries after O... didn't tell him of our splitage... will tell them both... some time.

Church was cool: a few old buddies were there – good to catch up with their goss (unless it involved them having a b/f or g/f, in which case I changed the subject onto the weather as quick as poss without being noticeably rude).

Did bit of sunbathing – is v hot n sunny.

Mon 18 July

Still haven't told them re me and O... Mum is still so pleased for me, and so enthusiastic re me actually having a b/f at last. Is easier to leave whole subject for time being.

Wish I had the guts to drive to his house... and that was insured on parents car, in case I ever GET the guts to do this.

Tue 19 July

3:21 pm

Just back from v painful experience. Dentist. Only a check-up, then a teeth-clean... but was still awful. Have always been scared of dentist visits... never even had a filling tho! The trick (says Mum) is to stay calm, by relaxing all body parts in turn... sort of switching them off, and switching your mind off to what's happening... and then focusing on something nice instead!

I was doing fairly well, reminiscing re the Prince Will thing... until I realised how much saliva I was producing. Thing is, have absolutely no idea how much other people produce when they're having their teeth cleaned, but sure I have tons more than them... bet they call me 'saliva queen' when I leave the room.

Notice that got all hot n sweaty in the chair... due to stress I guess, and raised heartbeat. Figure that raised heartbeat usually = weight loss.

If so, I ought to go thrice weekly...

Sat 23 July

Soz haven't written for so long, but nowt to report really. Life here a lot slower than at uni, which is to be expected I guess.

Height of excitement today... after tea, Mum asked if she could 'have a word' with me, which is an odd thing to say to your own daughter, who's living in your house and you can talk to (at) whenever you choose to (and she usually does choose to). Still, we sat in the lounge, and I waited. She didn't say anything for a while, just looked as tho she were preparing her speech, and needed more time to get it 'just so'. Kind of reminded me of whole 'gay email' incident a while back – when she actually thought I WAS gay... nightmare. Wondered what I had done this time...

Turned out I am destined to go to hell coz I say 'crap' now and then! She couldn't even SAY it in the end... had to write it on back of church newsletter, and point at it, so I knew what word she was referring to (when she said she had a problem with my 'swearing'!). She's overheard me say it on phone to Libs... at least twice I think (which isn't bad, considering we've spent many an hour yapping on the phone this past week!). OK, so guess I didn't really use this word before uni, but it's hardly swearing, is it? Must have caught it off Libs, but then she says a whole LOT of things, many of which would cost the NHS lots of dosh if Mum ever overheard as she would need years of care after the triple heart attack it'd give her.

Mums – don't you just love 'em?!

Said I'd try not to say it in front of her and Dad. She said this wasn't the point, as I shouldn't be saying it at all. I disagreed. We agreed to differ (well, I did – who knows WHAT she agreed to... prob a 24-hour prayer and fast on my behalf in order to deliver me from 'the "C" word').

Sun 24 July

I have taught parents how to play Uno – we play it a lot (oh, to be as retired and care-free as they are!) – I don't say the 'C' word when I lose, and Mum seems happy with this arrangement.

I force myself to say, 'Ccc…crazy!' now…
Well, it works for me.

Wed 27 July

Final day of BB! Even parents watched it with me (tho they had no idea who was who and what on earth it was all about).

The bloke with the cheeky grin and sexy muscly arms won… but then he would, wouldn't he. Oh to be the winner of BB! Oh to meet the supremely hot Dermot! Oh to be on front page of *heat*… AND get paid tons for it!

Dream on, gal, dream on.

Thur 28 July

Just been into town with Dad (he had to get some parts for his train set)… bought myself *What Not to Wear* (part 1 AND part 2 – they didn't look as tho they were books that could be separated from each other).

Let's see… Trinny has no boobs, just like moi. She recommends high-neck tops, like halternecks… hmm.
Why did no one tell me this BEFORE? Bah!
Have never really worn halternecks… must buy some asap.

Right. Moving on – the 'big bum' pages… they recommend hipsters – HA! Excellent – have got something right then!

OK, now on to the dreaded 'flabby tummy' that I have lived with in a love-hate rel for many years now… it loves me and I hate it! They recommend… NOT wearing hipsters. Huh? So I NEED to wear hipsters to disguise my big bum… but I MUSTN'T wear hipsters as they'll make my flabby tummy even worse?!

H E L P!

Part deux? Well, sorry – but some of those summer wedding outfits are just not on… even the ones they recommend! And

Short break there, due to Mum leaning over me/book, and commenting on what a lovely outfit the lady was wearing... (summer wedding, daytime, smart... the 'DON'T wear' page. Bless!)

Trinny looks fab in everything...

To be honest with you, Bob, I'd be a happy bunny if I looked ½ as good as Susannah does, let alone Trinny, the skinny cow. (I will repent of this statement at later stage.)

Wonder what O's doing right now?

Prob not deciding which one of Susannah and Trinny he looks like or would like to look like (I hope).

Wonder if he's thinking about me?

Or if he's wondering if I'm thinking about him, which I'm not...

(She lied.)

Mon 1 Aug

9:46 am

No no no no no!

Welcome to panic-ville.

Suggest you don't stay for long... IS V STRESSFUL HERE!

Nope – nowt to do with having now spent 2 weeks at home with parents (tho that is kinda stressful, but let's not get into that now).

Basically, I JUST NOW (mid my am super-large bowl of C Nut C Flakes) remembered that am booked to go to Soul Survivor this summer... which, according to my trusty calendar, is in, like, 2 weeks time!

Problem with this – I booked to go *with* O as he's doing a 'Living with alcoholism' seminar thing there. He booked us in not long after we got back from Romania... AGES ago... but I can hardly go now, can I?

We can't go together, anyway.

Hmm... who else is going... will just search brain a sec... ahhh, yep:

Duncs & Lauren (hope SS doesn't have same affect on them as S Harvest did – couldn't face it if they broke up again)

Fax

Sas

Not Libs (she said something re joining us for a day, but is unlikely)

Not Lydia & Jon (think they're dedicating time to... 'each other', whatever that means)

So, if I could go with the gang, and not just O, that'd be OK, would it not? Not sure if any of them will fancy transporting me there tho… will have to get some serious phoning/begging under way…

After have had one more bowlful… to give me strength in my hour of panic.

You still here? Thought you'd've hopped aboard the 1st train to sane-land! You really are a star, Bob, hanging around like this, despite my desperate ramblings…

Incredible wit/humour aside (mine, in case you missed it)… would so love to be able to go to SS with O… been to soooooo many Cn festivals etc in my time, but never been accompanied by b/f.

Was going to be O's greatest supporter – help him with seminar etc.
He'll be OK, he always is… wot about me tho?
I'm not OK. I miss 'im.

Tue 2 Aug

7:21 pm

Spent last ½ hour on phone to Abby. Nice to chat with someone re how PANTS am feeling – told her re convo with Sas, and how I finally decided to move my butt and go see O… only to find him long-gone. Her advice:

1| *Tell Mum and Dad – is wrong to pretend am still with O, as is lying.*
2| *Pray, ring O, say sorry, see what happens.*

She said she'd pray for me (prob coz she knows perfectly well I'm tres unlikely to act on her sisterly advice). Still, was good to chat. She seems to understand. NOT gonna tell parents yet tho – is too awkward. Mum will bombard me with questions till the day I leave for uni again – nightmare.

Will act on one piece of her advice tho – will pray. Perhaps will get divine inspiration re what to do.

Oh, and Abby lol when I mentioned Soul Survivor, saying it always made her think of Shepton Mallet (errr… coz that's where it is, in case you're a Cn from Mars/USA and are unaware of this fact) and that Shepton Mallet always made her think of TIMMY MALLET, and he really creased her up.

Hmmm… my sis – she has her moments.

Wed 3 Aug

Ooo Oooo Oooooo – just thought of totally fab made-up joke:

Q: *What do you get if you cross Tim Hughes with Shepton Mallet?*
A: *Timmy Mallet!*

Genius!
Must try out on ppl at SS (if I manage to get transport sorted, that is).

Sun 7 Aug

Church OK. Vic (pastor) did sermon on the golden calf at bottom of Mount Sinai... and how we shouldn't have any idols in our lives. Interesting. He said we should carefully examine our lives and ask God if we have any 'idols' that get in the way of our rel with him, and ask him to help us sort them out. Must do that sometime.

Seems that most of old church mates, who were around when I 1st came back home, have now gone off somewhere for majority of summer – 2 on some Cn thing abroad, I gone to London, so she can WORK for the summer (huh?)... Feel a bit Jude-no-mates. Still, did catch up with one old bud from youth group days... Mark.

Ooohhhh. Even saying his name again, after all this time, is a tad freaky.

WHY? Coz I used to fancy him tons – in fact, until went to uni and got all obsessed with Reuben... had desperately hoped that Mark was my one and only... my true 'Bob'. Course, he was never the slightest bit interested in me.
SO, quite odd to see him this am for 1st time (since me starting at uni).

We had good chat... from which I concluded that he's STILL not interested in me. Fair enuf... nice/hot as he is... he's still not O.

AND it is vaguely poss that I spent a good couple of years pursuing him, based on the verse:

'Mark the perfect man...'
(Psalm 37:37, KJV)

At least I've matured since then, eh?!

Had chats with another TWO guys actually (aren't I the lucky one!):

1| Des – *church student coordinator – just checking I received a Xmas card from him/the church, last Xmas. He smiled when I said I did, but then paused for a few secs, assumedly waiting for me to throw arms around him wailing, 'Oh and it really made my day... you're too good to me, you really are!' He swiftly moved on when I didn't.*

2] Jim – old youth group leader! (not that HE'S old, tho he's gotta be 30+ at least) He's the one that featured in my freaky dream, when I 1st started at uni... the dream that messed me up spiritually for several months!

Was v fab to see him... caught up with all he's doing in Uganda re goats n stuff. He asked if I was OK with God now, and told him I was. Couldn't help but tell him stuff re O tho. He said the same thing as Abby – that I should talk to him, esp if I have got apologising to do. He's so wise. I ½ wanted him to give me a direct prophetic word re me and O (that we'll get back together etc)... but he just said he'd pray for me, which he did (right then and there!).

Why can't people understand that I CAN'T just 'talk' to him coz it's too hard... coz he lives far far away... coz I can't face phoning/emailing him... coz I don't think I'd have the words to say if he were here right now?

Mon 8 Aug

Hayfever worse than ever... think all farmers in area have ganged against me, and are all cutting their hay TODAY... or whatever it is they do that has this effect on me. Mum is having to do an extra run to Tesco to stock up on tissues. Extra journey to Tesco is more of a big deal here, as is couple of miles away (no supermarket in our village!), whereas takes a matter of mins to get to Tesco from halls. Such is life. Mum doesn't mind – is v sympathetic... she's good like that.

Have run out of Winnie the Pooh tissues that O gave me.
Can't bring myself to chuck the empty box away tho... it sits on my bedside table; a shrine to things that might have been.
Hmmm... a shrine – that's a bit like an idol, innit? In style of golden calf as per Sunday's sermon? No. Surely not... is only empty box... is not like am worshipping it or anything.
Phew... had myself worried for a min there!

Still haven't touched a drop of the hard stuff since my vow of t-totalness! Is weird: I know I CAN, as am no longer doing it for O... but don't feel the need to. Perhaps I'm doing it for Pete... or even for myself (?).

Tue 9 Aug

9:12 am

Baaaarrrrrhhhhhh! Just walked into room to find W the P shrine (but not idol) tissue box... GONE!

Yelled to Mum re this... She said it was empty, so she threw it away!

Raced to the bins outside back door, but box not on surface. Really didn't feel like plunging hand into the wastage... Yuk! My shrine now crushed... prob squished between last week's soggy teabags and mouldy crusts of Hovis.

Trif.

10:34 am Odd. Was just havin shower, when Mum (not my fave person right now) shouted thru door that there was a 'young man' waiting for me in the lounge. Have quickly nipped from bathroom to bedroom, to inform you of the situation, for your info!

Only 'young man' can think of that it might be is Mark (the perfect man?), as he did mumble something about calling in if he had time. Hmm. Let's go see....

Post-young man I am on cloud 9. No, cloud 99... with thoughts of leaping on cloud 100 when it next passes by! I am in love. I am soooooooooooooo happy happy happy!

It was O.

Yep – right there in the lounge, drinking tea, munching on Mum's rock cakes... chatting with Dad re new additions to Dad's train set. I wandered on in... and there he was! I froze and considered fainting due to shock... Mum chirped 'Oh, how LOVELY it is for Oren to surprise you like this, Judith... well, aren't you going to give your b/f a hello kiss?'

O slowly and carefully placed cup, saucer/rock cake on Mum's new 'occasional table' (why do they call it that?) approached me, giving me light kiss on cheek, and little wink at same time, which I THINK said:

'I know they don't know we're split up... but I'll play along, just so as not to embarrass you, you daft gal!'

After enforced joint convo with my parents for an hour and ½ (!), we finally got time on our own. I apologised, and not coz people had told me to, but coz I knew I needed to. He apologised, not sure what for, but he seemed to want to, so didn't stop him.

He asked, v politely, if he could be my b/f again!

La la la la I'm so happy I could... do lots of happy things. La la la la la.

This is IT now... am going to be the most normal, open, honest g/f in history of g/fs. Am never going to try to be someone am not, or TRY to be anything at all! Just going to relax and enjoy our rel – get to know each other again, etc.

He insured me on his car this aft, so I can drive to and from S Survivor! Told him I'd never be able to do it, but he insists – says I NEED the practice! He's right, of course – always is. Might be OK if I'm down off this 'love-high' I'm on at the mo, which is sim to being quite tipsy!

'Warning: Don't drink/be on 'love-high' and drive.'

La la la la la... life is good.
Must go thank God for all this – he really is tops!

10:41 pm Parents are fine with O staying here until SS (in fact, are made up re this!).

11:03 pm Pssssttt... Bob... guess what? I love O! (Wanted to say this using little heart symbol, instead of the word 'love' but there ain't one on the keyboard... there's a gap in the market then... a keyboard with a heart symbol!)

Fri 12 Aug

Day 5 of love-high

Has all been so fab fab fab!

We've been down local village pub (coke and chips – just the 2 of us, and the locals... no rowdy students... bliss!).
Been for long walks – is v sunny/hot.
Even spent quite a bit of time with parents... they are somehow a lot more bearable when O's there too, prob coz I let him do all the talking, while I just daydream re our future:

1] *Wedding – big or intimate?*
2] *House – big or cosy?*
3] *Kids - how many? Names? ASAP after getting wed, or wait till we're older?*

Anyway, we're all off to beach for the day, so must dash!

Post-beach Ordinarily, am not huge fan of 'beaching'. Why? Coz:

1] *Sand gets everywhere – in food, in bags, even in box of Kleenex (and therefore... up nose)*.

2] *Screaming kids, whose families have set up 'camp' right next you. There should be laws forbidding this.*

3] *Stony beaches – really do feet in.*

4] *Soleros – too expensive compared with purchasing from Tesco.*

BUT, none of this bothered me today.

Had such a good time.

Mum had made her amaaaaaaazing coronation chicken, that we took in sarnies for lunch.

Most memorable bit: when O kindly offered to check my head for nits/scalp-zits. Still paranoid re nits, even tho have been nit-free for a while now. Was so nice to have him comb through my hair: v therapeutic – felt like a perfect moment, like all was well with us, and the world, and God etc.

Soooo hot. Swam in sea a bit (as had thorough shave yesterday, of all bits that were in need of de-hairing, in prep for wearing swimming cossie). Still, was only happy to swim if there were other people swimming further out than me/us.

Come on... have you SEEN Jaws?! Mr Shark always comes when there are happy yells of glee from kids, and groups of teenagers larking around. Then you see shots of people's legs dangling in water, like perfect shark bait. And then, Mr Shark gets the munchies... and it's bye-bye innocent swimmer. Kind of figure that, if Mr Shark DOES come along, at least he'll go for the people he comes to 1st (ie the ones swimming further out than me) and when I hear THEM scream... I'll have time to swim ashore, with all limbs still attached. Not a v Cn attitude I guess, but is only way I can fool myself into swimming without fear of sharks (Mr OR Mrs Shark... tho hard to imagine a female being that vicious).

AND I explained this all to O, as want him to know 'the real me'.

He just laughed, and said he had attack of munchies himself, and we went and bought ourselves Soleros.

Only 3 days till S Survivor!

Excited, but terrified re O's insistence that I drive there. Perhaps I can get him to change his mind... hmm.

V late Suspect O has been on phone with Fax since our beach trip, seeing as have just received the following text from Fax:

15 times as many ppl are killed by falling coconuts as by sharks

Now, why did no one tell me this before?!

Mon 15 Aug

7:21 am

Woke up to POURING rain… why today? Has been so sunny all last week!

Begged O not to make me drive… esp as so much rain… If he REALLY loved me, he wouldn't make me do it.

His reply was that it was BECAUSE he loved me that he was making me do it, otherwise I'd forget how to do it, never have confidence in my own driving, blah blah sensible-talk blah. Huh. Didn't help that parents were in complete agreement with him.

6:35 pm Well, we're here! Am currently in the 'cyber cafe'. Is queue of 6 people behind me waiting for their turn at computer, so can't be too long!

Drive here = OK.

Well, OK in sense that am still alive, as is my gorgeous passenger/co-pilot O. Not OK in sense that was terrified the entire way, and journey took a good hour, which is a long time to be terrified for! Body stiff due to keeping it continually tensed up. Glad I did it tho – must keep practising… it'll come naturally one day, won't it?!

Is still tipping it down. Not ideal circumstances in which to pitch our tents… but managed it eventually, with help of the others (who had left well early this am and got here before us):

Duncs & Lauren
Sas (not her b/f tho)
Fax

Fax says Libs might come tomorrow, but he hasn't heard from her in a few days, so can't be sure. ('In a few days'? They must be well in-touch… Will someone PLEASE tell me if they're an item or not, or I'll have to ask them myself!?)

Oh, and Reuben is here somewhere, we THINK. Last we knew, his band was due to be playing here, but he's not found us yet if he is here. Odd really, that he can come here and play in a Cn band, at a Cn festival… when he really does seem to have abandoned all things Cn this last semester.

Already been to a couple of good seminars... Duncs made copious notes throughout one on something to do with worship... no doubt this will form the basis of his next 'this-is-the-most-important-thing-in-our-Cn-lives' talk at BURP.

He'll need to find the book to accompany his talk too... the book that if NOT read, will lead to eternal, and probably fairly instant, damnation. He's always looking for the 'latest' Cn thing... we've had name it and claim it, health and wealth teaching, healing, 'the future', fasting... the list goes on.

He doesn't just 'recommend' Cn books... he all but says that when we reach those Pearly Gates, we'll be quizzed on whether or not we've read the book, and failure in this area will lead to refusal of entry.

Still, at least he knows what's going on, I guess... the geek (bless 'im).

Oohhh – have been on here longer than had planned... bloke at front of queue giving me rather non-Cn looks... and he has tattoos on his left arm, so must depart asap, and meet others for main worship doo-dah.

Ttfn Bob!

Tue 16 Aug

6:04 pm (in cyber cafe)

Eeee by gum. Life at SS is well cool (tho not literally, as is v hot again... rain has ceased!).

Libs turned up, just as we were tucking into breakie (beans on toast, or something representing it, cooked by Sas)! All v pleased to see her. She seems to have enjoyed her day so far, and is staying on till late, so that's a good sign.

Around midday, she said she wanted to cook... but, when I mentioned us getting started on lunch, she said

'Naaaa babe... I meant me!'

As in, she wanted to sunbathe.

So Libs, Sas and I devoted much time to this. Lauren said she preferred to stay out of sun, due to skin cancer etc. Typical over-paranoid geeky attitude, imo. Is there a Cn book re 'not sunbathing'? If she talks to her dear Duncs about it long enuf, he's bound to be the one to find it and inflict it on us in near future.

I devised a 'rotating' plan, to ensure that all body parts got equal exposure to sun's tan-giving rays. It involved quite a lot of moving around, and trying to hold awkward positions for long periods of time, esp in attempt to get backs of calves done... but was convinced it would all be worth it.

Was it? Nope. Libs and Sas achieved their goal of being cooked to the 'well done' stage... I am still more 'medium rare'. In fact, in steak terms... they are rump steak...
I am still cod steak.
Typical.
I don't even LIKE cod.

Post-painful shower Just popped in to ask you – you know how sometimes you THINK you're not sunburnt, but actually you really really are? Well, just had shower... and was v ouch ouch ouch... am cooked, bigtime!

Shower + sunburn = agony.
(Now that would've been a USEFUL equation to have learnt in GCSE maths!)

Libs seemed to enjoy the main eve mtg, tho she did find it rather odd... but then you would, if you'd never seen anything like that before, I guess. She said she could see God meant a lot to all these 1,000s of people. Felt like asking if God meant anything to HER, but held back. Mustn't hassle her re whole thing.

Wed 17 Aug

9:47 pm (in cyber cafe)

Lauren started up convo re skin cancer over breakie (Pot Noodles, chicken and mush flave, water boiled and poured by O). Have to admit it was pretty freaky... she sure knows a lot about it... Did you know that a lot of people get skin cancer on their EARS as that's a place where people often forget to put sun-tan lotion? Not sure I want skin cancer. Can hardly believe am saying this but, after a good few summers devoted to the hobby, am going to be a sun-worshipper no longer! It's factor 60 for me now... bought some from site shop earlier, and have already applied liberally, inc EARS (tho O had to wipe some of it off afterwards, as it got more stuck ON ears than absorbed into them, if you can picture it).

Hmm... even tho we pooled together the food we all brought... it seems to have run out this am, which is rather unfortunate as still got 3 days to go! Perhaps we slightly underestimated the appetites of camping students, who do have rather a tendency to graze from dawn till dusk! Only option is to buy food from food vans. So much choice:

pizza
doughnuts
pancakes
Mexican
potato wedges and dips
ice cream
toasted sarnies
freshly baked baguettes
crepes
etc

Wonder if can manage to sample it all before we leave? No harm in trying! (Apart from cost, that is... a pint of orange juice is £2!)

Have had 3 lots of ice cream and 2 Soleros today by way of 'dessert'... Bring it on, I say!

Post-Nazarene gig Hmm. Had to come back to report this. What to say? Most bizarre. When Reuban told us, a while back, that Nazarene were doing a gig at SS, we kind of assumed it would be an evening thing, in one of large venues, as per gigs of the Tribe etc. We'd all thought it rather odd that couldn't see any evidence of them doing a gig in the programme.

Then he saw Sas in 'Dreggs' earlier today, and said they were performing at 5:30 pm. We checked out all the main venues from 5 pm, in search for Nazarene, but no luck. Sas wondered if she'd got the time wrong... We ended up in the food court (obviously)... which is in same place as outdoor bandstand.

Dead on 5:30, Reuben appeared from nowhere, leapt up onto bandstand, and started to announce that Nazarene were about to perform their latest song. Was all v odd – the bandstand is for wannabe bands after all, not ones that SS have booked to do a REAL gig, surely?

Can't say the crowd were that responsive in general... We all cheered loudly tho – someone had to! The band joined R on the bandstand, and were just getting into the 1st few bars of their song... when

BANG BANG BANG BANG
'All to-ge-ther!'
BANG BANG BANG
'E-ven lou-der!'
BANG BANG BANG BANG

The drumming workshop, that had, to this point, been confined to the safety of the venue opposite the food court... had just decided to go walkabout, on some kind of 'hey guys – look – we're drummin' march. They were loud. Not really my thing but, more to the point, you totally couldn't hear Nazarene.

Some residents of food court began to laugh, in a not v Cn way... You could see that Reuben and co were having a tough time of it. Got a bit worried that Reuben might get attacked, as happened to Robbie W once, just as he started a huge gig. Was sooooooooo embarrassing. Felt really sorry for them, but also helpless... was nowt we could do.

Reuben held out tho. Waited till the drummers had marched well past, and started again. Fortunately (v v fortunately), they were well good, and got massive cheers at the end! They went on to perform 4 more songs!

Reuben looked well-chuffed when they finally left bandstand... had obviously been a triumph for them. Does he really believe in what he's singing tho? Who knows.

We had to leave pretty sharply, as Nazarene were followed by a v poor Justin Timberlake attempt. There were cheers, but think they might've all been a variation of the word 'STOP!'

Lauren has lent me some of her 'fake tan' spray. Have sprayed it all over, several times, but still look cod-like. Perhaps it's past its due date or whatever.

Huh. Still, O will love me anyway, so mustn't grumble.

Thur 18 Aug

12:56 pm (in cyber cafe)

Woke up around 7 am (impossible to lie in when you're camping, or at least when you're sharing a tent with Sas, who has to pop off for shower/grooming session at crack of dawn!). Sat outside tent for a bit, reading a book that Duncs thrust into my hand late last night, and commanded me to read. (Is about idols n stuff – how to spot them, how to get rid of them etc. Hmm, that description makes it sound more like a book on rat-catching! Is quite boring, but decided to humour him by reading it, just until the others got their acts together and got outta bed/sleeping bags.)

Next thing I knew, there was an almighty scream, only about 2 metres away from where I sat. It was Lauren, who had her head poked out from her ½ unzipped tent (she has a tent to herself, as she likes to go to bed earlier than Sas or I, which figures).

Her scream was most def aimed in my direction. Instead of answering my puzzled look with words (that are usually called for, to give clarity to such occasions), she just waved her arms wildly at me, pointing, doing geeky, goldfish impressions with her mouth.

For a sec I wondered if I was starkers, but a quick check reassured me that I was fully-clad, in my trendy Powerpuff PJs. A further glance down at my arms was far far LESS reassuring…

Streaks.
Orange ones.
Lots.
Looked kinda diseased.
Orange streak disease (OSD).
Is there such a thing?
There is now.

Licked hands and began to scrub off… Sas must've spilt her foundation on me, surely?
Nope.
OSD wouldn't budge…
Hmm.

With mild horror dancing in brain, with vague thoughts of applying fake tan last night, I had quick peek at legs…
Yep. Just the same.

By the look on Lauren's face, could tell that my *face* must also be infected. Would've been almost funny, if it had happened to anyone but moi.

Lauren obviously felt tres guilty, as she wasn't laughing. She tentatively asked if I'd followed the instructions on the spray can.
Instructions? Only geeks look at them, don't they?

Oh, to be in the land of the geeks, and to know how to apply fake tan without giving oneself OSD!
Sounds like STD – must stop saying it.

Apparently, you spray it on v lightly and evenly and it appears over the next 4 hours or so. Lauren says it usually lasts a couple of weeks on her!

So, can either sunbathe again, to fill in the gaps left by streaks, in attempt to look normal... but this could cause skin cancer... or can spray MORE fake tan on, in the gaps...
No... is all too much.

Will leave it like it is... will be an effective reminder to me (and to most attendees of SS) to read the instructions!

Am kinda OK re whole thing now, but the next person who says to me, 'Hey, Jude... why's your skin all orange n streaky?' will get their personage hauled up to balcony of the skateboard park, and chucked OVER balcony, into the scary skateboarding frenzy below (not by me, of course... will have to locate that tattooed bloke who was behind me in Internet queue the other night... he looked scary enuf).

Hot goss: Duncs said we ought to pray mightily for Reuben, as he spotted him snogging some lass, who scuttled off when Duncs approached Reuben (sensible lass). Then, when Duncs innocently asked R her name, he said he had no idea!

Typical – same old Reuben.
Sad, really sad.

8:32 pm Just popped in to tell you that O's seminar was FAB!
Was so proud to see him up there, at the front.
He gets to wear a double ticket thing round his neck, being an important speaker and all. I'm going out with an important Cn speaker... life is good.

Guess there were about 50 or so there... Had no idea so many people were interested in 'Living with alcoholism'. During the question time thingy at the end, was fairly obvious that lots of them had lived with (or are still living with) alcoholics, just like O did. Scary.

O was great. Such a natural. Could easily be on the God Channel.
He did get a bit choked up, when he described stuff his dad used to do, and all, but then that's to be expected, I guess... brought tiny tears to my eyes too... how he coped I'll never know.

Even my nightmare streaky skin didn't stop me from standing right next to him at the end, handing out leaflets while he chatted to people etc.

If only Mum could've seen me/us!

Fri 19 Aug

SS summary

Personal failure (fake tan aside): telling at least 4 separate ppl my 'Timmy Mallet' joke, none of whom laughed, only 2 of whom even bothered to groan. I tried to backtrack, taking them thru it slowly, trying to explain to them WHY it was so funny... but somehow made it worse.

Best purchase: a Cn-fish toe ring (already have toe ring on 1 foot – did quick survey of all mates present, as to whether or not 1 toe ring per foot was a bit OTT... they all agreed that it was... Bought it anyway – sometimes you just have to trust your own instincts in such matters, and it's so CUTE!).

Best mtg: the one have just come from, when they said stuff re putting God 1st in your life. Cried a lot. Most people did. Even O! Was nice to share it with him. Felt even closer to O during the mtg... God has blessed me so much by giving me him! How could I NOT put God 1st?!

Quite a few people 'went down in the Spirit'. Saw some lass right in front of us, being prayed for, looking a bit wobbly... so quickly shifted myself and bag etc in front of O, to make way for the potential toppler... only to find I'd moved myself IN the way, as that's the way she then fell... good job O intervened and sorted it out. Am clearly not 'in tune' with this kind of thing, which makes little sense, seeing as we had it all the time at old church... must be getting rusty.

Memorable moments: sitting outside our small cluster of tents until the early hours, looking at the stars, laughing, praying, yapping, sorting out the world... and also doing all this with random people that passed us by. God bless random people!

Funniest of Fax's facts: sitting round a table in food court, fairly late one eve, with a bunch of other dudes, we were all tired, and anything and everything made us laugh... One bloke complained his coffee had gone cold... Fax lept in with:

'If you yelled for 8 years, 7 months and 6 days, you would have produced enough sound energy to heat up one cup of coffee.'

You had to be there.

A pizza flave vest top

Sat 20 Aug

8:39 pm (home)

YOU will NOT believe this.

Hmm. That sounds like am about to give you some morsel of juicy goss, which am not. This is far more serious. In terms of seriousness… it's… well, it really is.

This is something I found out last night, after my trip to cyber cafe to write to you.

Something I can still hardly believe is true.
People just don't GET themselves pregnant, do they!?
Well, PEOPLE do, but not STUDENTS.
Well, students DO, but only when they sleep around a lot.
Not when they've done it ONCE.
With their b/f… their CHRISTIAN b/f.

Lauren.

I know. Sounds like a bizarre, if rather cruel, joke… but is not.

Sas? Wouldn't have expected it, but would've made more sense.
Libs? Would've expected it, tho think she is on pill (or WAS – she doesn't seem to bed so many guys of late, if at all, come to think of it).
Me? Would've been divine miracle/2nd coming… as still 100% virgin.
Lydia? Logical – is married and all, tho would've expected them to wait till degree over and done with, but…

LAUREN??

They told us (v tearfully, both of them) it had happened 'just once', when they 1st got back together, after the S Harvest split. They hadn't meant to, it just happened. They REALLY regretted it, repented etc. Then left it with God, they explained.

Twas only a week or 2 ago they found out… they wanted us to know… so we could pray for them, as they have NO idea what to do.

We all hugged and prayed A LOT.

Makes me cry again just picturing her pale face, all messed up with tears. When I gave it more thought, they HAD both been rather quiet during SS, kept themselves to themselves a bit... but that's what couples usually do, so hadn't given it a 2nd thought. Wish I had.

Feel so useless. Yeah – know I can pray, but that's hardly gonna SOLVE anything, is it? How could God let this happen anyway? O says these things just do happen sometimes, and that they'll be OK, in time... but still, geeky as they are, I feel so so sorry for them both.

Is not as if Duncs can locate Cn book on this subject, sort it all out, and move on... what's done is done... there's a baby involved.

A baby!
Man, is all so freaky.

Sun 21 Aug

Another thing I didn't tell you re SS – drive home was only mildly less terrifying than journey there. Stopped off at services – had a little cry in toilets, when using hand-dryer (made in Honeypot Lane, where my Nan used to live – I miss her).

O drove back to his mum's this am... he says she needs him until he leaves for uni again, and I know he's right, gutted as I am that we can't be together for next few weeks.

Can't stop thinking re Duncs and Lauren. Will they get married now? Course, they will ... they've got to, haven't they? Hmm.

Not sure things were supposed to be this way by end of my 1st year... By the end of 3 yrs perhaps, at a push... but not one.
It's all so Jerry-Springer-style dramatic, but in a tragic way, rather than a funny one.
Am gonna give Lauren a ring now, see how she is...

Sat 3 Sept

1 week till am back off to uni, and the unknown world of '2nd year'. Am moving into house 2 weeks early so can earn some much-needed cash at Fusion. Also, O is going back to his uni house early, so it means we can spend lots of time together!

Sat 10 Sept

7:41 pm (new house!)

Wow – haven't written to you for whole week!

Most days have involved:

1| *Making the most of Mum's fab cooking, and wishing she could make loads of meals and freeze them, so I can take to uni house, and defrost on daily basis for whole of this semester.*
2| *Playing (and winning) Uno with parents… think I've really started something: they are talking about getting some sort of electronic Uno version for their anniversary pressie! Still, they are retired.*
3| *Ringing/emailing O… several times a day, for rather extended periods of time.*

Have also rung Lauren a few times, just to check she's OK.

Today was moving in day… is great to finally be here now. House stinks of poo, but it'll be fantastically fragrant by the time the others move in, courtesy of moi.

Can't wait for them all to join me now… so we can all be housemates together – like shipmates at see, like oil-personages (?) on an oil rig… like the new extended family we never knew we had!

Is sort of nice to be here by self tho… can stick Kylie on REAL loud and 'become Kylie', in the style of 'becoming Kylie' (or other sim pop celebrity) on MTV, without the actual make-up crew, wardrobe, special effects, choreographer etc. You get the picture tho.

Is just getting dark now, and am getting a bit freaked re thought of actually being here on my own throughout the night. Will ring O and ask him to get over here, if he's in Bymouth yet.

Not good with the dark.

Mon 12 Sept

Hmm… fishy.

Went to Tesco today. Not an unusual habit in itself, but was kinda different to last year in that am now having to think about actual MEALS, as opposed to just snackage. Am a receiver of uni refectory meals no longer. This is it, Jude – the real world.

The real world smells of fish!

Had never actually been to fish counter in Tesco before... till today. Thought it just had to be done... REAL food shoppers do such things, one assumes. If they don't, why would fish counters exist? Not to improve the aroma of Tesco, that's for sure. Had encountered the odd fishy whiff, whilst passing the counter before, but is soooooooooooooo much whiffier when you're standing right in front of it.

All those little fish looking up at me... with fishy eyes. (Why can't they chop the heads off? Is so grim.) Eyes made me quite nervous – felt like was just starting at Fusion again – got all paranoid. Bought some salmon fillets (fillets turns out to be the lingo for 'without bones', according to the fish-counter-guy). V healthy – lots of Omega 3 oils, or whatever.

Also went down 'cleaning' aisle for 1st time ever... Like being in another shop altogether – a whole other world I hadn't realised existed in the land that is 'Tesco'. V odd, and also smelly, but at least is hygenic/fresh smell... and not mingin' fish.

Tried to suss out what cleaning stuff will buy 'collectively' with housemates in near future, but was all a mystery to me... housework not really my bag, baby. Sure some of others will have more of a clue (won't they?).

Tue 13 Sept

12 midday

O has stayed v v late the last 2 nights. Kind of odd, the 2 of us having this big house all to ourselves. Nice tho. We watch TV, chat, all the usual stuff... until I can stay awake no longer (2 am perhaps?) and then he goes, knowing I'll fall asleep instantly, and won't be awake long enuf to be scared. I even do my teeth, take out contacts, get into PJs etc before he goes, so I can lock door behind him, then dash up to room and leap into bed pronto... and pray like crazy until asleep. Is working so far.

Is Freshers' weeks – this week and next. Freshers are annoying me already... some of them hanging around library this am, not really working, but just yapping... so perky and KEEN... I'm thinking:

'Guys, calm down – it's only uni, not Hollywood.'

Still, guess I was just the same this time last year, bless me little student socks.

Library? Me? Yeah, but only went to meet O there... he's the studious one, not me, don't be silly!

Spoke with Pete on phone earlier – he was on phone to O and asked to speak with me, which was cool! Seems more natural to chat with him now. Well, as natural as it can be to chat with someone who's still got another 5 months' sentence to serve. Will be so weird for him when he comes out. Guess he'll need to find a job. Shouldn't be too hard, he's an intelligent guy. But then, like O pointed out the other day... Who wants to employ an ex-con?

At least he'll have O.

1:21 am Uh-oh. Not good. Awkward. Freaky.
O's just left. He stayed late, as has been our pattern.
What HASN'T been our pattern is to get... you know... physical.

Well, we've snogged, of course... but not done much else. I haven't really had to monitor the situation too much, firstly coz I'm not really that desperate for sex or anything (am I?) and secondly coz O always pulls away when it gets a bit heavy, like one of us puts our hand on the other's 'danger zone' etc... guess I'd assumed he'd always stop things, so there was nowt to fear.

Suppose we haven't really had the opportunity to get too physical up till now, being in house all alone. In halls you're always so aware of people in surrounding rooms, and walking along corridor etc. Even in O's house there were usually people around, or at least you knew that people COULD appear at any time. We just never went that far.

But just now...
well...
clothes were undone.

Only briefly, and not a big deal, I guess... but is still more than we've done before, and don't feel good about it. Know O was horrified at himself/us. We were both the guilty party. Problem is, can't help thinking that it could happen again... and what, if he DIDN'T pull away as fast as this eve... what would happen? We wouldn't do IT, I know.

Well, I think I know. I know we don't WANT to do it. Well, we WANT to do it, sort of, but it would be wrong to, so we're happy to wait, blah lie blah!

Happy to wait? Is anyone really happy to wait till marriage? Bah.
Is it really such a sin to have sex before the big M?
Course it is.

Hmm.

Now I'm all on tod, and wide awake... left to play with such thoughts, which aren't conducive to falling asleep peacefully. Can hear drunk people in street...

'SHUT UP, drunk people (prob freshers)... Am trying to get some shut-eye, and am scared enuf without having to consider whether you're gonna break in...'

Ohhh... really shouldn't have had that thought, that's really not helped.

Have just stuck TV on again... Kind of feel safer with background noise, even if it is Graham Norton repeat. It also blocks out sound of drunks, which is an improvement. If this room/house smelt less like poo, it would help all the more.

Wed 14 Sept

Had done so much cleaning/sorting/reorganising in house this am that couldn't help slipping into *Cribs* mode (as on MTV) when O came round after lunch...

'...and here we have the pool area, where me and the band like to hang out...' (Puddle in cupboard under stairs – source currently unknown.)
'...don't you just LURVE this walk-in closet... I can just about fit all my outfits in here, on a good day...' (Smallest bedroom, currently stuffed with boxes of my clothes.)
'...and finally, I asked my design team to give the kitchen a fresh and funky look, something that really reflected 'the real me' – I think you'll agree they've done me proud!' (80s-style pukey, brown n yellow flowery stuff... or is that 70s? I dunno.)

O had hysterics! We both did! We've prob seen too much *Cribs* in our short lives – must cut back. He left, speedily, after we'd had some grub (spag bol, courtesy him), shouting over his shoulder that he wouldn't collect me from work, and was I OK to get a taxi?

Hmm... taxi = more than a few pennies, a fact he is WELL aware of.

So why the avoidance?
Am guessing it has something to do with last night.
Not looking forward to coming home to empty house... freaky.

Post-Fusion O obviously forgot that he's a man who tends to keep his word… he was there waiting for me, on dot of 1 am! Turned out he HAD been a bit freaked out by last night's, erm, activities… We had good chat re whole thing. Was great. At least we feel same way – freaked! Both keen to avoid mistakes we'll regret. Esp in light of Duncs and Lauren situation. Both keen to stick to God's advice re sex avoidance etc. Is cool.

Well, WAS cool… but somehow, at 2:30 am… we were watching some pants film on Five… and then… well, the next thing I knew, my vest-top was no longer on my personage. In fact, it was v OFF my personage, in style of being ON the floor, residing IN empty pizza box (ham n pineapple flave).

It was O who suddenly pulled away, saying, 'NO! Sorry Jude… sorry!'
And plonked himself in armchair, leaving me alone on sofa.
I re-applied vest-top ASAP, and we just stared at each other for a bit.

I couldn't help thinking, 'What if he didn't pull away? How far would I actually GO before he stopped me? Is he testing me by doing this, to see how sluttish I am?'

But no, from brief convo that followed, seemed that HE was the one feeling sluttish. He said he'd never done 'this sort of thing' before, and couldn't understand how he could let it happen. He looked close to tears. He started saying something about that bit Paul (in Bible) says re 'what I hate, I do', but didn't have much to add after that.

We were both rather lacking in convo… due to shock, I guess.

He left just after this, and I am AGAIN left trying to go to sleep, with all this racing round my little head. Trif.

Thur 15 Sept

Got rather 'involved' with a phone-in on *This Morning*: 'My partner's sex-mad – what can I do?' Wondered if O was sex-mad. He's sooooooo holy in most ways – v close to God, v SC&O Cn etc. All this is not in keeping with his style, but then he's a bloke, and blokes like sex, it seems, esp according to phone-in… Those poor women!

At least we've ADMITTED we've got a little problem here, and need to be careful. Mind you, we DID the 'admitting' stage, assumed it was all dealt with… but my vest-top has still managed to acquire tomato stains since then, courtesy of Pizza Hut. Hmm.

Oooohhhh… just lookin at calendar – only a month to go to O's b'day!

He'll be 21! Wow – sounds so far away from me, a baby still at 19.

What to get him tho? Shall I opt for practical or funky? Boring (but safe) or totally 'out there'? The latest Adrian Plass book springs to mind (we are both super-de-dooper fans) and is not as if can afford tons. Hmm. Will ponder on this at work, which am due at in, errr, 20 mins.

As it takes me 23 mins to walk there, really ought to get going now! Adios.

Fri 16 Sept

Lydia rang this am, during today's phone-in: 'Empty eggboxes and their uses'. Prob a v necessary interruption – mustn't get too dependent on daytime telly after all.
She invited me over for a bit. Said yes. Haven't wanted to bother them since have been back, as all a bit awkward, knowing that they've got probs, and them KNOWING that I know about them having probs etc... but seeing as she actually asked me over, I went.

Twas good. They seem pretty cool now. Not all over each other or anything, just... relaxed. Relaxed with each other. That's what it's all about, I reckon. Jon said that the main thing which had helped them, other than talking/praying with Mike and Jane... was learning to 'communicate' with each other. Thought this an odd thing to say, as they've been married for nearly a year now... they must communicate all the time! Then remembered what Amos had said at BURP earlier this year, about marriage being all about communication. Hmm. If both married couples say this is important, then what singleton am I to argue! Perhaps is all to do with HOW you communicate or something.

Sat 17 Sept

O and I spent some of today at Mike and Jane's. Well, Mike not actually there, but Jane was and... Radox, with her new-improved look! Can hardly believe am saying this, but had her on my KNEE for a while (Radox, not Jane). She really does look so... clean and NICE... just couldn't help myself. Maisie would've been proud!

Almost asked Jane re whole 'physical' thing between me and O... but didn't coz O might not want me to 'share' our prob with others... and coz is such a freak-city thing to discuss anyway.

Late Success! We managed to keep our wandering hands to ourselves for whole eve... played Uno to keep things clean.

Thinking about things, after he'd gone, caused me to locate the box containing Oscar's sex books, and have a quick goosey-gander at them. Not sure what I was looking for... something that told you how NOT to have sex I guess, but no joy. Books are only pro-sex, and the pictures give me more thoughts than I can handle right now. Have put them away again... well away!

Hmm... such 'unusual' image overload means I need to visit kitchen for my 2nd Pot Noodle of the day (beef and tomato flave).

I WILL start cooking properly soon when the other housemates show up. Honest!

Sun 18 Sept

Couldn't concentrate during sermon... kept thinking about Duncs n Lauren... and how on earth they're gonna cope with this semester. Also thinking about me and O, and whether or not it could ever happen to us (getting preggie).

The prayer time was good tho. The minister said we had to really focus on one thing to pray for, for 5 mins, in silence. Really focused on me and O, and asked for a solution to our little 'getting out of control' problem. Didn't get any divine answers, but felt good to have discussed it with God.

Are Duncs n Lauren actually married in God's sight now, or not?

Yapped with Lydia during coffee. She's getting Jon a number plate made with 'I luv jon' on it, for his b'day, next week (not for his car, just a novelty one!). She says it's the kind of cool thing he always gets her, and that his sister always gets him, and that his sister's b/f always gets for her... and so on.

I see what's happening here. No longer is it fashionable, or even acceptable to buy something 'average' for your loved one.

CDs? Out.

DVDs? Out.

Box choccies? Out.

Smellies? Out. Even trendy ones, like cK one.

We're now in an age of super-trooper cool pressies... has to be original, has to REEK of cool-ness. Numberplate is FAB idea, but has been done now, so is a no-no. Must get brain in gear re this... must get the best pressie EVER!

Post-eve service We were well-shocked to see Sas turn up for eve church, even if she was ¾ hour late! Eve church isn't really her thing... not that she often comes to am church! She didn't look too happy tho, nor did her b/f (nice bum) who came in with her. Wondered if they'd had a row or something. Saw myself having words with them afterwards, re 'communication' being what it's all about.

She made a bee line for me when service over... but not in a hi-Jude-how's-your-summer-been kinda way. More in a

'WHERE'S THE KEY?!'

kinda way.

Ah. Whoops! She rang me yesterday to remind me to leave the key to house under large stone by front door, so she could let herself in this eve, knowing I'd be at church. I didn't. Totally forgot.

Tried to laugh it off, and said we'd really have to get each housemate a key cut ASAP... but she wasn't really in the mood. When her and I got back to house (after telling/snogging our blokes goodnight) I had visions of us watching chick-flicks n getting involved with some serious snackage well into the early hours etc, but she just said she wanted to sort her room out, and remained distant and grumpy until I could finally bear it no longer, and went to bed.

Hmm. Not quite how I'd pictured it... Still, is early days yet.

Mon 19 Sept

Overslept... came downstairs to find that ALL remaining housemates had arrived in the last few hours. Sas had clearly told them the events of last night, as I was greeted with:

'Jude, we really do need to get keys cut for all of us.'

'Jude, I'm going out soon, but will NEED to get back into the house around midday, as I'm bringing a mate back here... If you're all out, the key WILL be under the stone, won't it?'

'Jude, I hope you've repented of your mistake, and have asked both God's and Saskia's forgiveness.'

(Last comment came from Duncs, obviously.)

And I'm thinking, 'Hey dudes, LIGHT-EN-UP!'

Is not like I did anything seriously wrong, like pinch the nice bum belonging to Sas' b/f, or steal Fax's book of 'useless info' (that one assumes he has). No, I just forgot to put the key under the stone. Big deal!

Did apologise tho, to keep the peace.

Made me cross with myself for not ridding the place of poo smell yet, which might have put me in a better light with them all.

Duncs' 2 mates – Dan and Neil (who I kinda know from BURP, but not really that well) have got the 2 rooms on the top floor. They seem OK. Kinda geeky and quiet... but I'm all for 'quiet', having lived next-door to Marilyn Manson for the past year!

At least it's a house full of Cns. Cool!

Tue 20 Sept

All change! Dan has just decided that he's NOT going to live here after all! Turns out he was originally hoping for a room in another house, nearer to where he works, but it just didn't work out. This am (while I was out getting 6 keys cut) he got a call to say that circumstances had changed, and that there WAS now a room in this other house. So he's off! Is worse than *Big Brother*... we hadn't even had a chance to vote!

He says it's all OK tho, coz he's got a mate lined up to take his room here, in our house. They're doing the swap today!

Bizarre!

Haven't seen our newbie yet, but have put his key on his bed, so at least HE can't be against me for being the 'key' baddie, like the others are. Huh!

Keys aside, I've mainly got sex on the brain.

Not in a Joey and Chandler kinda way... more in a 'Huh? Help!' kinda way.

Lauren was over quite a bit yesterday. Her and Duncs are closer than ever, but perhaps in a more 'scared/tragic' way than before... when it was just about being in love. I look at Lauren, and can't help thinking, 'Wow, there's a baby inside you!' She seems so much more grown-up all of a sudden, like a real 'woman', as opposed to a 'girl' or just a genderless 'student'.

Sex is so... so... dangerous. People rave on about it, but look at what it does... Libs had an abortion, and now Lauren's pregnant.

Oooohhhh... saying that makes me shudder, thinking of Libs meeting

Lauren, esp when Lauren is really showing... not sure Libs would handle it v well. Hope Libs keeps up with the counselling this semester. Would be good if she could come off the Prozac too, but that might be asking too much of her. I dunno – is all beyond me. Surely these are 'grown-up' problems... not things I want to even have to THINK about, let alone DEAL with.

7:32 pm O and I just back from meal at Abby n Amos'. Good to see them again. FAB to see Nat and Eve (who now has hair just like her Dad's, a mass of super-tight black curls – cute!)... They have grrrrooooooooowwnnnn in the summer hols!

Nat insisted on sitting up to tea with his full Spider-man costume on... but eventually agreed to take the 'hood' bit off, as no food could enter his mouth otherwise (as Spiderman doesn't have a mouth, for some reason!).

We got yapping re Lauren etc. They can hardly believe it either. Was just wondering if it was at ALL possible that Abby and Amos 'did it' before marriage, when Amos launched into their 'family planning' story, which went something like:

'We both went to the family planning clinic, a few months before we were due to get married. We wanted some advice, for when we got married – we wanted Abby to go on the pill, but needed to know more about it. In the consultation room with us was the doctor, the nurse, and a student doctor – quite a little party! After asking us all our details, the doctor said: "... and what form of contraception are you using at the moment?"

'And we said, "None."

'And he looked at the nurse, who looked at the student, who looked as confused as the other 2. They were probably thinking: "If this couple don't want kids yet, why aren't they taking any precautions?"

'So then we sorted it all out, by saying: "We're not sleeping together yet: we're waiting until we get married, in a few months."

'Silence fell on the room. The doctor stared at us, then at the nurse and student, who stared back at him, and then us. Then, in a kind of odd unison, they, all went, "Aahhhhhh – right, I see."

'It was as if we'd said we were from the planet Mars. Nothing could have shocked them more. It will probably be a story they tell to their colleagues, and even their kids: "the couple who WEREN'T doing it! How UNNATURAL!"'

Nuff said then – A&A clearly were virgins till the bitter end... I mean, till the wonderful new life of 'marriage'. Figures. Like they've ever done anything wrong in their lives. Huh?

Don't know why it annoyed me so – is not like me and O have done it. Not like we're likely to,
or are planning to or anything (are we?). Family-planning-story rules tho – will have to tell it to MY kids one day!

Amos also said how awful the whole AIDS thing is back where he comes from (Kenya). Nightmare. Sex can be such a nightmare.

Bog-roll bickering

Wed 21 Sept

3:35 am

Yeah, tis a tad late to be awake... am well aware of that. I did in fact go to bed at the v sensible (boring) time of 11 pm, seeing as twas the time that O left (he's decided he doesn't need to stay so late, now I am not being left alone in the house).

However, is now 3:36 am... and I am again awake. Reason?
EMINEM... V V LOUD!
Not that Eminem's here in person, as far as I know, but that his oh-so-melodic voice is BLASTING down to my room, from the floor above... the top floor, where I have a strange feeling the new bloke has just moved in. Time to introduce myself...

Trif. Back again. New bloke = 'Gaz':

1] Not a Cn,
2] As friendly and polite as Eminem himself,
3] Fluent in using the 'f' word – somehow manages to slip it into every sentence, like it was the law or something,
4] DEAF (or pretending to be... music is so LOOOOUUUDDDD!!!).

Didn't really hit it off. Not sure my Powerpuff Girl PJs really helped. He said he'd turn it down, and he has, but now it's just 'loud', as opposed to 'v loud', which is still not fun at this time of night. Might have to buy earplugs tomorrow.

Post-breakie Admittedly, Gaz was slightly nicer to me and the others over breakie... still not sure him being here is good idea tho.

Haven't done much today so far. Think have got my room how I want it now... boxes all emptied and stuff distributed accordingly... there's only so many times you can rearrange stuff! The others are all out. Where? Dunno. Busy. Busy with their busy lives. Even O said he was 'busy' this am (seeing his dad on his own, and then doing some study or something). Feel a bit down. Not sure why. If anything... feel a bit homesick, for old house, parents etc. This is tres odd, seeing as I got over being homesick around Easter-time. Perhaps is coz was at home for so long over summer. Moving into house is rather like leaving home all over again, sorta. Is not that I think I'd rather be back home, than here… just that I don't feel… settled, that's all. Bummer.

Post-row Hmm. Just had stupid row with Gaz, re bog roll. I hadn't gone looking for a row: it found me, or rather… Gaz did.

I happened to notice that the bog roll was the wrong way round, in BOTH toilets. Being the person who'd bought it and put it in both loos, I knew that it had started its life the correct way round, and that somebody had been messing with it. Asked the only 2 housemates currently on board the starship, Gaz and Fax.

Fax denied all charges of having messed with the bog roll. Gaz, however, raised his voice somewhat – said that HE had changed them, and put them the RIGHT way round, as they had been the WRONG way round initially.

Fax got all confused, and demanded to know how come he'd never heard of a 'right' and a 'wrong' way to hang bog roll… so we all visited loo on 1st floor, for a little demonstration.

Clearly, the correct way to hang it is so that it's hanging AWAY from the wall… It's easier to tear that way, imo. Gaz said this was a load of BEEEEP (toilet-related word, how kind of him to keep his swearing topically relevant!) and that it ought to hang NEAR to the wall… this was what he'd grown up with, and this was how he liked it. Started to point out that there were 6 of us living here, and we all had to consider each other etc… but was interrupted by Fax, who blurted out:

'I think you're both mad… I always take it OFF the holder anyway, so it really doesn't matter which way round it hangs!'

Gaz and I, while having our differences, were not prepared for such a clear violation of standard toilet protocol. United, we turned on this… this… weirdo, and I began to ask WHY on earth he did that, when I was again interrupted, but this time by Gaz:

'Naaaa – dun wanna know… too much info dude…' and skulked back off to watch *Murder, She Wrote* in lounge.

Think I would've preferred one of Fax's facts re lavatories, over and above learning of his toiletry habits.

Where are your annoying facts when we really need them Fax, eh?

WHY DOES he take it off the holder?

Thur 22 Sept

I can't say that one thing has gone disastrously wrong in this house and upset me. Nope, coz the fact is that THREE things have gone wrong, and I am one v unhappy bunny right now:

1] Sas, who turns out to be more domesticated than had assumed, boiled some eggs yesterday, as she is rather keen on her egg sarnies. She said I was welcome to have one if I wanted, with my lunch. Took one from fridge, but decided I'd rather have it heated, and sort of mush it up a bit on some toast... seemed like a good plan at the time. Popped it in microwave... 28 secs later... POP! Exploded egg, all over innards of microwave. Had to spend 15 mins getting it clean, before the others saw it. Grim.
2] The shower is so pants... it's painful to have one – the water sputs out at you so hard and fast... and I NEED to have showers, so this is bad news.
3] Had phone call from nice lady today, asking if I fell in the range of between 18 and 49 in age. When I replied in the affirmative, she went on to ask if I was aware that 1 in 9 women get breast cancer. No, I wasn't... but how FREAKY is that. She then said that she could offer me protection – think it went along the lines of me paying them £5 per month, and then, in the event of me getting cancer, they'd give me £9,000, then £500 per month after that, for a year, then £100 for every night spent in hospital... The policy would also provide for my kids, in the event of my death.

All v depressing.
And to top it all, I have to go to work now.

Sorry to be such a Moaning Minnie, but am really pee-ed off now, coz... ahhh... door...

Was Fax, with a friendly reminder that we've got lots to do to get the BURP stall sorted for the Freshers' Fair tomorrow... it will take most of the day... We start at 9 am!

Have been trying like stink to avoid freshers at all cost. Not sure really want to greet 100s of them, and persuade them to join us at BURP. Still, will be cool to nab all those new Cns wanting to join BURP, I guess... mustn't be negative. Please God, make me less negative!

Fri 23 Sept

Libs just called by! She's moving into her new house today. Is so odd not to be living in same place as her… perhaps this is another reason why I feel homesick. Maybe it's halls I miss, not home! Was real good to see her. She IS gonna keep up the counselling, so that's cool. She got here at 8 am (don't think that gal ever sleeps) so felt bad when I had to leave at 9, to sort out the BURP stall thing. But she then said that was fine, as Fax had told her all about it, and she was coming with us to help. Dawned on me then that she'd come round to see Fax more than me, I think. Charming! They MUST be going out, on the quiet. Not seen any signs of anything physical tho. Hmm.

Spotted a vast amount of last night's washing-up in kitchen… shouted up to Neil, who I'm sure was responsible for it… he shouted back about hoping it was going to decompose naturally, in time… or biodegrade. Blokes. Nightmare.

9:32 pm Am so so knackered! We worked like the busiest bees this side of Honeyville from 9 am thru to about 2 pm! The stall thing we came up with was pretty cool tho – worth the effort.

Lydia & Jon helped too, as did most of the committee. Lydia said (from her experience as ex-BURP president) that Freshers' week was 'make or break' for so many Cn freshers. There are 100s who sign up for BURP, then you never see them again!

Why do people do that tho… and wot do those naughty Cns get up to, if they don't actually come to BURP, or a nearby church? Hmm… obvious I guess… all down to 'beer pressure'/sex, imo.

Basically, we spent most of our time giving out the cool tracts Fax did for the P Will gig, and trying to get people to sign up for BURP. Shame we couldn't have enlisted the help of P Will… he really was a superb crowd-puller.

The Gideons had a stall on other side of hall, and were giving out Bibles. At 1st, I thought they hadn't got a hope in hell of getting any response from freshers… who wouldn't want to look 'uncool' by accepting a Bible off an old bloke with white hair, dressed in a suit. But bless 'em tho, after a bit they had more business than we did! Don't know how they got so many punters at THEIR stall, but something they were doing was working! They were even chatting with the freshers! Bizarre!

After a while, they went to the enormous palaver of moving their stall to be next to ours, after Fax and the chief Gideon-man had been yapping about working together etc. They turned out to be a cool bunch of old dudes, really all-out for God too. Wonder if this is what O will be like when he's 70?

Oh, and we were also inviting freshers to our 'thing' tomorrow eve. Fax is doing it, and doesn't need our help, he says… It'd better be good, that's all I can say.

Anyway, having been on feet for most of day, my feet are well aching. Fancy a long hot shower, but can't hack the pain… will go and fix myself a meal instead…

Bad idea. For some reason, Duncs had bought some cream (a whole pint!) and it was on kitchen table. For some reason, I managed to knock it over, whilst passing the table. For some reason, one pint of cream, when knocked over… turns into 10 pints of cream… Soooooooooooo hard to clear up… went everywhere. Am so tired and still quite down… made me cry. Then I could hear Mum's voice in my head, telling me not to cry over spilt milk. Then my own voice in head told me that it's not milk, it's cream… and I could cry as much as I wanted to, so there.

Hmm… guess is still a dairy product tho… and similar to milk… whatever.

Am back in room now, bawling eyes out. Is v late, but will summon O here, as need him. Don't remember feeling depressed since going out with O (not including when we split up)… didn't think it'd ever be possible to have b/f, and fab one at that, and be so depressed. Will ring him now…

All sorted! Well, not sorted, but O (who came over) reminded me that it was my special TOM (how sweet – he remembered), and all this was probably related to this, and would be gone soon. Hurrah! Still feel pants, but at least I know why. How come it took a bloke to point this out to me… you'd think I'd have the hang of my monthly bout of 'iffy' emotions by now. Huh.

Just when I was starting to feel better… he asked if I had any tights. Is not like him to ask about my underwear, so this threw me a tad. Then he said that if I didn't, he could use some of Sas' tights. This was even worse… now he wanted the tights for himself! Arrrgggghhhh… a b/f who wears women's tights!

But no, turned out he wanted a pair of tights with which to fix the shower, which he did. He unscrewed the showerhead, descaled it, and cut a patch from the tights to insert in it, to stop it from spurting out the water so hard. He's so good!

OK, so I have complained about the shower on more than one occasion in last few days, but he's still so good to remember, and to be such a fab DIY person. I love him!!!

Sat 24 Sept

10:32 am

Just had long long hot hot non-stinging shower… scrummy.

11:42 pm Fax was right – he didn't need our help this eve with BURP 'welcome'/outreach thing. We got a whole lot of punters, which was great… and unexpected! About 150 of us in all… BURP hasn't been this big in ages!

We started off with an 'extreme sport'… which turned out to be a v dangerous game of Giant Jenga that Fax had borrowed from F&Ferret. Not sure it actually qualifies as an extreme sport, but it went down well!

After some serious mingling, Fax did short talk… on anacondas!

I know, doesn't sound like your usual thing… and it wasn't. V clever tho – he said lots of bizarrely interesting stuff re anacondas, then made some comment to us about our life at uni, the choices we have to make, how this relates to our rel with God etc. All good stuff – could see the freshers lapping it all up… he was a big hit!

Don't ask me exactly HOW he linked anacondas to us/uni/God, etc… is hard to explain.

Facts re anacondas that I remember:

1] *They can eat deer, or humans… whole! They then sit and digest them for several weeks. Wow – imagine that… several weeks of no hunger pangs/no need to plan meals/zero trips to Tesco etc… bliss!*
2] *13 males wrap themselves around one large female to mate, for up to 46 days, each taking turns.*

Nuff said.

Some people (like Fax) are just so good at doing talks… don't need visual aids, bells n whistles etc… have captive audience from start to finish.

Think he's improved a lot since last year – he'll be the next Mike Pilivachi by the time he leaves uni!

Libs (who was there) said it was the best Cn talk she'd ever heard and that, if lectures were like that this year, she wouldn't have to skive them!

Great to feel both encouraged AND challenged at the end of it… and to learn so much re the life of anacondas!

Sun 25 Sept

Jewellery. New jewellery. On a finger. On a female hand. Left hand. A ring.
Mine?
Naaaa – don't be an idiot.
Lauren's. Lauren's got a new ring…
She's ENGAGED!!!!

Is wild! Well, guess not, in the circumstances… but still, not sure any of us thought it would be so soon. Mind you, guess in 4 months time she'll be having it (baby) so not much time to waste. Guess we all thought they'd prob get married… they've got to, haven't they?

They didn't make a big deal out of it – no announcement from the front of church, just brought it up during coffee after service, and flashed ring around a bit. Both looked genuinely happy… Lauren really is 'showing' now, in a big way! Everyone knows re pregnancy at church. Duncs says some people he used to chat with a lot haven't said a word to him since they found out… and have been avoiding the 2 of them big time. Poor things.

Some visiting speaker did sermon on 'not having idols'. Sure we had a lot of this kinda thing at church earlier this year… is getting a bit same-y. Keeps making me think of *Pop Idol* – who might win the current series… and how come I'M not on it, doing my funky thing!

Saying that, it did make me think back to the stuff that was said at home church in the summer, re golden calf and stuff that can act as the same type of thing in our lives. Hmm. Also took me back to S Survivor, where they said stuff re 'putting God 1st' on the v last eve.

I'd really taken it all in, and resolved to read Bible every day from that day onwards (currently only read it about once a week… slap-ie wrist-ies… but I AM v busy, but then guess I still find time to watch fair old bit of TV, hmm).

Was gonna pray loads, and ask God to clear out anything that might be getting in the way of our rel… but is odd how all this kinda thing shrinks to nowt, or almost nowt, when S Survivor is all behind you, and you're back in the real world (if uni can be classed as the real world!).

Must focus more… but I don't have any idols, do I?

I am putting God 1st, as much as am able… must put more effort into the rel tho… must must must… he's done so much for me – look at how he looked after me over the last year, allowed me to go thru all that doubting stuff, without letting me drift off altogether. He's fab.

Lectures start tomorrow… back to normality then.

Mon 26 Sept

Spent lecture deep in thought: What will I do when I graduate? What career exists that involves v little work, but pays lots n lots of £££££££££?

Talking of £… Gaz has proposed to the house that we don't 'bover' getting a TV licence, as he really can't afford it, even if it is split 6 ways! He reckons we'll get away with it no probs. Fax's reply was that you can get fined £1,000 for not having a licence.

That shut him up! Even split 6 ways… that's a fine of… errrr… £175.66 each (or whatever… is not like am doing a BSc or anything).

Not wanting to miss an opportunity (while all 6 housemates were, for once, in the lounge at the same time)… Fax added that you could be fined the same amount of dosh for knocking a policeman's helmet off. This led into a deep discussion re the difference between someone knocking one off accidentally, and on purpose… which was brought to an abrupt end when Sas realised *Countdown* was starting, and told us all to 'sush-up or gerr-out!'

But really tho… how could anyone knock a policeman's helmet off ACCIDENTALLY, for goodness sake? Huh?! How are they held on? Do PCs balance them precariously in the hope of getting them knocked off – perhaps they get a commission on fines!

Almost did some study (1st assignment of the semester, set by Prof Carr today – he wastes no time!) to escape Carol Vorderman's yawnyawn face/voice in *Countdown*… but retired to kitchen instead, to participate in multiple bowls of cereal with Fax and Neil (living in house just as damaging to diet as living in halls, darn – it!).

5:31 pm YIKES!! Just back from freaky 'parking practice' with O, in Tesco car park. Not too good. He wanted me to park in a space where there was a car EITHER SIDE of me!! I preferred to have a car on only one side of me... or, better still... NO cars for at least 5 spaces either side of me! Call me a wuss... see if I care.

No BURP this eve, as we're all a bit knackered due to freshers' fair (Fri) and freshers' welcome thingy (Sat)... esp all that extreme sport!!

Watched *Pop Idol*, which we'd recorded, avec Sas dans her chambre. Almost told her re my band-related fantasy, but didn't... think I'd have to know someone for a good... errrr... 50 years, before I told them that. Course, you're the exception, Bob... I tell you everything, so here goes:

I'm at a Cn festival/event/thingy (like S Survivor, par exemple) and it's the 1st day of it. A real cool band (like The Tribe) is due to do a gig on the v last evening. Prob is, they're one dancer/singer short and need to find someone. By some bizarre (divine?) turn of events... they spot me in the crowd and ask me to fill in!

They spend those few days training me in the dances, vocals, etc... sort my clothes/hair/make-up etc. Then it's the gig itself... I'm FAB... they decide to take me on full-time... I spend the rest of my days being cool, in a band, touring the country... no, THE WORLD... and make trillions of ££££ in the process (which I'll give to charity, of course... well, some of it, anyway). The end!

But don't tell anyone, Bob – is a tad embarrassing. Is not like I can actually sing or dance that well really... but still... a gal can dream!

Tue 27 Sept

4:47 am

Arrrrggghhhhh!!! Am wide awake at naf time again... not due to Eminem this time tho... but to, well...

Woke up... room was well-hot, as was I. It was the smell that got to me the most tho... not the normal poo smell of the house (that I am learning to live with, but really wish I wasn't) but a kind of evil, unfamiliar smell... the smell of death?

I sensed someone was in the corner of the room, where my beanbag is... but it was too dark and, even by straining my eyes, I couldn't make them/it out. Gradually, a faint amount of light fell on the corner in question, and could just make her out... a woman, all huddled up... black... v gaunt... eyes closed... dead?

I froze, not sure who she was, why she was there... and whether or not she posed any kind of threat to me. Mainly, she reminded me of those starving African people you see on adverts, asking you to give money to some charity or other... but worse. Much worse.

As I watched, her eyes slowly opened, and she looked directly at me... a fearful, desperate look... like she'd seen the worst life could dish up, and more. Admittedly, I was scared/confused... but my lips didn't seem to want to move, even tho I wanted to ask her... well, I dunno... something.

It was then that I noticed she had something in her lap... a small dog? No, a child. This was where 'death' came into it... the child, her child (I assumed), was dead. I stared at the child for quite a while, willing it to produce even the smallest flicker of movement... but nothing. Looking back at her face, I realised she was whispering something, over and over... I swung my legs over the bed, and stood up... as if this would help me hear better, somehow. Hear her I did:

'Help me Jude. Help me Jude. Help me Jude...'

Her eyes were fixed on mine... over and over she whispered those words... without pausing...

and then she was gone, or rather... I woke up (for real this time)... standing right by my bed, exactly as I'd been in my dream... but she was gone, as was the deathly smell.

Am writing this to you now as am WELL too freaked to go back to sleep again. Am all hot and stressed (stays v hot in this room all night, even with window wide open!). Want to erase image of her from my brain... she's kinda hanging around in there and, if I close my eyes, she's as clear as can be – her and her dead child.

Or DO I wanna forget? I am feeling really affected by this... like things are making sense now that didn't before... there are people out there who need help. My help! Is all v well to talk about the starving millions, and put 10p in a box someone shakes at you in the street, to help them... but no one says what to do when one of the starving millions comes directly to YOU, looks you straight in the eyes, and asks YOU for help, eh?

I almost feel that if I go back to sleep now, it'll all be gone in the am... faded away, classed as a nightmare, and nothing more. But it is more... it's real, or at least that's how it feels. Perhaps is God urging me to get on and DO something for people who need help. Will get on and ask him now...

Thur 28 Sept

Spent most of yesterday in a bit of a daze... partly coz I didn't get back to sleep after my dream/experience... Read some of James instead, re helping orphans and widows etc. Important stuff. Made me think of Romania, and all the plans I had when I was there: to change the way I live, only spend the bare minimum on myself, and give the rest to people who need it.

Couldn't really focus on anything at all yesterday... Feel the same today... Need to talk to someone about it.

Have talked to O, obviously... he says it is prob God's way of nudging me in right direction, and that he has this sort of thing on his mind a lot – whether he should give up degree and go work full-time in Romania... whether it's really RIGHT to spend money on a CD, when others in the world don't even have enough to eat. I know he thinks about this sort of thing a lot... it's not like I haven't listened, but perhaps I haven't really taken it on board so much, up till now. All that stuff which was said at BURP earlier this year re world poverty and our responsibility etc... I keep remembering little bits now... like pieces of a jigsaw... and all the time, the face of the woman sort-of haunts me... like she doesn't want me to forget... like I need to make some decisions about my life.

I know this all sounds a bit dramatic... it was only a dream after all... but it was just so real and so... I could almost FEEL her pain... like it kind of transferred across to me... well, not fully, as I have no idea what it's like to lose a child due to lack of food... but I've never felt that CLOSE to someone suffering before, ever.

Off to work now... can't think I'll be much use to them in the state I'm in. What's it all about anyway? Why am I earning money? To help pay for my education? Is that what God really wants me to do?

Fri 29 Sept

Had really been looking forward to having little 'outing' to the shops with all housemates, to choose cleaning stuff, and a few bits and pieces we need for kitchen etc. As it worked out tho, Neil, Gaz and Duncs all declined, leaving only me, Fax and Sas. Fax then said he'd rather leave us girlies to it! Huh – charming!

So Sas and I set off together, with strict instructions from the rest of the gang to get something... ANYTHING, to rid house of poo smell.

Sas didn't take our excursion v seriously tho... could tell she just wanted to get it over with, so she could meet her bloke and go clothes shopping before her next lecture. Whatever I mentioned as something we just MIGHT need to buy... she grabbed off the shelf and stuffed into the basket. We were done in ½ hour!

Still, was also glad to have a bit of time for my own shopping... ended up in River Island, sussing out the halter-necks (that you will remember came highly recommended by Trinny and Susannah, for people, such as myself, with no boobs). After about what seemed like a month of looking, I found one I actually liked... and joined the queue. Twas a super-long queue... as there always seems to be anytime I am in a clothes shop, and actually want to buy something. From queue, I watched the gals go in and out of the shop, taking stuff into the changing rooms, asking their buddies if stuff suited them, complaining at the price, but then queuing up behind me to buy it anyway...

And it suddenly dawned on me... I DON'T NEED THIS!

I don't need a new halter-neck at all. OK, so I need a top of some sort, but not one with this price-tag, it's just wasting money. Sacrificed my place in queue (even tho was about to get served, at long last) and exchanged it for a black top, that was just £8, rather than £20... and joined the END of the queue, for the 2nd time today.

Did a bit of shopper-watching again... it passed the time. And then it hit me once more...

I DON'T NEED THIS!

OK, so I thought I needed new top of some sort, as my old ones are rather 'last year'... but they're still wearable... in some parts of the world they don't even HAVE proper clothes... why don't I send THEM £8? Huh? WHY? Might £8 have saved that woman's kid from dying?
I put it back.

How can I know where to draw the line between what I WANT and what I NEED?!

10 rabbits and a lasagne

Mon 3 Oct

Poo smell still at large... is the 1st thing that greets me each am... why won't it just go away and leave us alone?

Is me doing BURP Bible study this eve... have been working hard on prep re it for past few days... Is on 'pure religion' (as per book of James) etc. Want to 'use' my suffering woman dream to make a difference, in some way. OK, so most of them will have heard this kinda thing before, but some of the freshers might not have. Perhaps I can help them to see the world more clearly... stop 'em from spending 3 years obsessing about what THEY need (like I have been) etc.

Hmm.

My prep includes a pile of acetates, with scary pics of starving people, some handouts to fill in, a game (to get people 'involved' with the topic), a video clip from a charity that works in 3rd-World countries and so on. Has been quite an effort (for a lazy minger like myself)... but is all done now.

Post-BURP Did not quite go according to plan. Had everything ready. Fax started by saying... something... but it was all distant mumblings to me... she came back to me again: the suffering woman and her dead kid – right in front of me. Tried rubbing my eyes and blinking, but didn't make any difference. Was kinda like having flashbacks, I guess. She just kept appearing, with that deathly whisper: 'Help me Jude. Help me Jude...'

Suddenly realised that Fax had stopped talking, and that everyone was staring at me. He must've just said something like '...over to you then, Jude', but I hadn't heard him... only her. I looked at the group... the majority of the old gang... a fair few freshers, who were clearly impressed by Fax (and his anacondas) the other eve and had come back for more. There they sat, in their £90 trainers, whiffing of £35 perfume/aftershave, fiddling with their mobiles that took photos, sent emails... and would prob cook you a 5 course meal if you pressed the right buttons... what could I, Jude, give to them?

A 'talk'? An insight into what it's like to suffer? How do I even know... it was only a dream? WHY on EARTH do I think I can change anything... I can't even change myself... I'm just as bad as every one of them... we're ALL selfish, ignorant, greedy, etc... here in the... what was that statistic Fax mentioned ages ago... in the world's top 20% richest people.

They were still staring at me, and I was still staring right back at them... willing some opening words to come out, but they didn't.
Then she was back... her face, and her voice... so clear, so painfully clear.
I broke down.
Head in hands, shoulders heaving, tears upon tears upon tears upon tears.

O put his arm around me, but it didn't help that much. After a bit I managed to sit up straight again, and have another look at them... all in their own little worlds, and not one of them, not one of US caring about the real world. Fax asked if I was alright... I said I was, and picked up my 'plan' for the eve, scanned over it...
and screwed it up in a ball. If my audience were confused before, they were def confused now!

Knew the only thing I could do was to tell them about the dream, about her... which I did. Not just how she looked, but all the details I could recall, and her dead kid, and her desperate plea for help. Was well aware that it might mean nowt to most of them, but wanted to 'share' it, just in case it/she might make a difference. I had my eyes closed for most of it, as I really didn't want to cope with everyone staring at me while I was still crying. On finishing, I opened them and looked around. Several people were crying, no one was fidgeting or whispering... everyone looked deep in thought.

Was tres relieved when Fax suggested we use the rest of the time to pray in 2s, re what I had said, and what we ought to do about it... I wasn't going to argue with that.

Tue 4 Oct

Was in town with Libs n Fax... who were unwilling to help me hunt for a b'day pressie for O (no idea why, apart from the fact that I had mentioned it MIGHT involve popping into every shop in town)... but agreed to meet me in a few hours for lunch. I said, 'Right, meet you later in McDs then.' which was greeted by the blankest of blank looks you could ever imagine.

Turns out we don't 'do' McDs now... we go to Wetherspoons instead.

Seems like we all graduated to W Spoons while I wasn't looking (mustn't knock it – might be the only time I graduate in my lifetime!).

Deep thought: If it was McDs in the 1st year, and is W Spoons in the 2nd... where do we hang out in the 3rd year? Jamie Oliver's restaurant in London?! Huh?

Joking aside, didn't feel too comfortable spending dosh on a meal out, what with all these thoughts re world poverty etc... but felt a bit better when found out that Fax only wanted a pint, so me n Libs could take advantage of the '2 meals for £6' thingy.

Opted for chilli con carne... smashin!

Had no luck finding anything for O... only got a week and 5 days to go... H E L P!!

Wed 5 Oct

1:30 am

Rang Abby earlier. Told her re dream, and embarrassing BURP thingy. She said her and Amos have thoughts re chucking it all in to go abroad and help, somewhere, in some way. They've been thinking about it for quite a while, apparently.

Amos knows of some needy communities back in Kenya, near where he used to live. Abby said they could sell their house and go live/work there, for good. She didn't even think the kids would mind... that it might even be better for them to be brought up over there, away from the Western ways of the world. Hmm.

Kinda hope they don't go tho... would miss them and kids too much.

Unless me and O went out there too, when we've finished our degrees... but what would we DO? How could my degree be of slightest bit of use to starving people? Huh?

Would I actually WANT to give up the luxuries of living over here?

Questions questions... sorry, Bob... is probably doing your head in!

Must go now as soooooooooooooo knackered after work. Was near to grabbing mike from Fusion DJ and commanding everyone to wash their own glasses from now on, as I'd had enuf!

Thur 6 Oct

Guess who's gonna be a bride? ME!!!!

OK, not really giving you the full picture... am gonna be a bride smaid. Still, bet that got you wondering, eh?!

Lauren asked me just now. We had a bit of a heart to heart actually. Even tho I know her quite well, don't really think of her as a friend, which sounds cruel... but we're just so different, or at least that's what I'd assumed, up till just now.

She knocked on my door, all out of the blue, saying Duncs had popped out to buy more cheese (for their beloved cheese n marmite sarnies... is it OK for preggie women to eat these? Will their offspring be born with an addiction to them?) and had suggested she hung out with me for a bit.

I tried to start off a convo re babies, thinking that she'd leap at it... but she looked a bit freaked, so I gave up. Then, just as I was wondering whether to change channels (from *Sex and the City*, to *The Office*)... she came out with:

'You think I'm a geek, don't you?'

Just like that! With no prior warning whatsoever... what was I supposed to say?!

I needn't have worried... she had a lot to say, I only had to listen (and switch TV off altogether). Essentially, she said she sometimes wished she could be like me (!) which completely freaked me out, as NEVER would have imagined that anyone would want to be like me. She said she knew she was rather geekish, but that she didn't know how to change, and wasn't even sure she wanted to... she didn't want to not be herself!

According to her... I am attractive, confident, and can have any friends I choose to (according to me, this is absolute PANTS, but didn't say so). On further thought tho, I could see she had a point... when compared to HER, I did seem that way. It was just that I continually compare myself to those trendier, hotter, cleverer, than myself... and thus have a fairly low (v low) opinion of myself.

Not sure this changes anything really, apart from that am flattered that someone is actually jealous of me... that's gotta count for something! Perhaps everyone is jealous of someone, whatever they're like... even the queen! Even Matt Redman!

At end of her speech tho, she said how much her and Duncs loved me, and how they wanted me to be her bridesmaid! Was so touched… we had a little hug, and cry. I feel for the 2 of them so much… it must be so hard. Getting married ought to be the happiest day ever… and theirs will be sorta tainted, by the fact that their baby is due. Not ideal.

Still – got tons to sort now… my DRESS for starters… she says I can help to choose it, as it's only me and Duncs' little niece that are the bridemaids. Am SO excited!!

It's on Dec 20th… Lauren will be well huge by then, but they want to do it before it's born… she'll just have to have a massive dress I guess! Perhaps she could borrow the tent me and Sas shared at S Survivor.

Fri 7 Oct

Forgot to say, we've got a new lecturer, just for 2 lectures per week. He's called Prof James, and is darn sight hotter than Prof Carr (which isn't hard – most of male population are darn sight hotter than Prof C). No, really, he's like about 30 or something, and well into surfing/snorkelling/water-skiing etc (how much do these guys get PAID?). I know these details re his life outside of lecturing, coz he does tend to go on about them somewhat. (Tho I don't see any of female students having a prob with this – he has rather sexy accent. Italian? So perhaps he is Italian? Dunno.)

Up till today, I'd thought him well cool.
Up till today.
Today, he handed me back my assignment… 42%.

Now, I'm no genius, but I usually get more in the region of 50–60%.
OK, to be honest, I don't always fall in this region, but if I don't, Prof Carr gives me a pretty detailed account of where I went wrong/how I could have improved it etc.

Prof James, however, seems to think that writing 'poor' next to the mark is sufficient. I, however, don't.

1st thing Mon am gonna give him wot for.
Told Libs this, who said this was unlikely to happen,
so I said it WOULD,
and she said it WOULDN'T,
and I said IT WOULD,
and she pointed out that WE DON'T HAVE PROF JAMES ON A MONDAY!
Huh.

Sat 8 Oct

BURP was cool... just a social really, as haven't really got to know freshers v well yet... we asked everyone to try to bring a mate, pref non-Cn, promising them it'd be just chat and snacks. Felt kinda chuffed that I wouldn't have to go to much effort to find a non-Cn, once I realised that Libs was coming. Freaky thing was... she turned up with HER housemate!! Gonna have to get me a more genuine non-Cn mate... is she slipping onto our side?

Sun 9 Oct

Managed to grab a few words with Mike after church (he usually goes to the C of E church on a Sunday, but was preaching at ours today!). Told him re suffering woman dream.

He seemed to know where I was coming from, which was great. Said that there was a guy doing the BURP Bible study, a week tomorrow, talking about 'holistic mission', and I ought to take note of what he says as it will probably be of use. Didn't like to say to Mike, but 'holistic' mission sounds a bit iffy to me... rather like holistic medicine or something... hmm...

Mon 10 Oct

Hurrah! Have at LAST found cool, and affordable, pressie for O. It OOZES of originality...
10 RABBITS!

'But, Jude, where will he keep 10 RABBITS?' you politely enquire, 'and would he really want them anyway?'

Oh, Bob, you are full of questions today... don't panic, man... they're not real!

Well, they ARE, but he won't see them... they will in fact be sent to people in Malawi who could really do with them! World Vision... found their website just now... sorted!

He'll get a card to say that 'his' rabbits have been given to a family. Will get him a bar of choccie too (a fairly traded one), just so he's got something to enjoy for himself (and that he can share with his fab g/f!).

BURP Bible study OK... best bit was when tons of people came here afterwards, invaded our lounge, and demanded a film. Jon and Duncs were sent out to get video (Blockbusters is just down road = tres handy). They returned with…

Chitty Chitty Bang Bang.

There were groans all round… some of the freshers in particular did NOT feel that they'd made it this far, all the way to the big wide world of uni… to watch a kiddies film.

Jon insisted we'd love it – it was his fave film as a kid. Even geeky Duncs looked a tad worried.
Still, watch it we did…

It was FAB! Not sure we've all had such a laugh in ages! All joined in with great gusto to the hearty wholesome songs… the lads all fancied 'Truly Scrumptious' (but we let them coz she is smashin') and the gals all 'ahh-ed' at the cute kiddies (all except for Lauren… but think she was just well tired, being preggie and all). Even O's feet were tapping in time to the music at the v end!

Think some of us even cried at moving moments… what more could you want in a film?!

Is a new plan we've got now… to watch a musical each week, after Mon eve BURP. Jon is in charge of selecting the film, as he did such a good job with this one. Lydia seems v proud of her hubbie… bless!

Finished off the eve with a mass game of Uno (don't ask how we did that… would take too long to explain!). Cool. A cool evening. Even think those freshers are alright now… strange how things move on… Can hardly believe I was a tiddly fresher not that long ago!

Tue 11 Oct

2:37 pm

Right, off to give James a slice of my mind now…

Post-slice giving Right, am back with my slice still in tact – he didn't turn up to our arranged meeting. You know what? Really don't care. If he doesn't care, then I don't either. Not a v Cn attitude, I know, but is how I feel right now.

Occurs to me that Prof Carr is actually not as bad as people (like me) tend to make out. OK, so he's old and boring, but he really knows his stuff. Not only does he know it, but he seems to want US to know it too! Guess that's what being a good lecturer comes down to – actually caring whether or not your students are taking blind bit of notice re what you're waffling on about. Hmm.

Almost feel like giving Prof Carr a massive bear hug when next see him.

(But won't – rumours spread well fast on campus.)

Wed 12 Oct

Had just got in after seriously yawnyawn lecture, and was approaching the kitchen (the room I tend to head for 1st, on entering the house)… when heard voices inside, and hesitated, just in case it was something private (and I could get some juicy goss!).

Twas Libs n Lauren. Kinda panicked… had been meaning to keep the 2 of them apart, as much as poss, as not sure Libs could really handle Lauren being preggie, esp now she's really showing.

A peek thru the gap in the door revealed a pile of cheese n marmite sarnies on the table, that Libs was heartily tucking into, but Lauren wasn't touching (perhaps Libs has converted to C&M sarnies, instead of Cn-ity). Lauren was crying and seemed to be in the process of ripping up a baby mag, that I think Duncs had bought for her earlier today. Libs, despite a large mouthful of sarnie, was trying to stop her, and in the end came out with:

'What happened, doll, with you 2 having sex, like, was wrong… not what God intended… but it happened, and you've said sorry, and he's forgotten it, ain't 'e? So now there's no need to resent this baby or to think it's a sin to have it… a baby is what God's all about… new life, celebration. There's EVERY reason to celebrate what's growing inside you… a person, a personality. God doesn't want you to be like this. YOU gotta get knittin', babe!'

She then grabbed a ruler from her bag, and a particular scrunched up page of mag from the floor by her feet. She uncreased it, saying: right, his head should now be about 'this' long. Lauren didn't look, but stared at the floor instead. Libs reached over and gently tilted Lauren's head toward the ruler… 'See… this long… how cute is THAT?!'

Lauren looked for about a minute, deep in thought, then replied, with a smile emerging on her face:

'What about his legs tho... and how do you know it's a 'he' anyway?'

Ahhh... thought I'd creep upstairs and leave them to it. Started to do so, but Libs shouted thru, 'OK, you can come in now, Jude... someone's got to help me eat all these sarnies anyway!'

Was real pleased that Lauren was feeling better about things, baby-wise. Kinda jealous that Libs sorted it all out – it should have been me who spotted her lack of interest in the baby etc, ME that said all that... not Libs, who isn't even a Cn... well, not officially, is she?!

Together we consumed the mound of sarnies, whilst using sticky tape to do a rough reconstruction of baby mag. Lauren seemed a lot happier. When she popped to the loo (which she does a LOT now), Libs had a turn at crying, holding my hand with one of her hands and the baby mag in the other... how she could say all that stuff to Lauren, I don't know.

Can't get over how unselfish it was of her to put Lauren 1st and say what she knew she needed to hear, even tho it couldn't be at all easy for her. I felt tearful when I saw Lauren cry... but Libs crying is always guaranteed to make me weep buckets. I wish I could help. I really wish I could help. I told her this, but she said that me listening to her and crying with her always did help, a bit.

Must go to work soon... the glasses are calling!

Sat 15 Oct

Is getting v nippy... is almost like we've had one week of autumn, and now it's winter! Bizarre. That's England for you, I guess. Trif. Good job have got O to keep me warm!

Is his big day tomorrow... hope he's ready for his rabbits (who I have already named 'Flopsy, Mopsy, Cottontail, Flopsy 2, Mopsy 2'... you get the picture. He's gonna love 'em!).

Sun 16 Oct

6:34 pm

O went home not long ago – just as *Home and Away* was starting, I think. WHY have I sent him away on this, his b'day? Coz I am preparing a meal for

139

him, here, for the 2 of us… he's coming back at 8! Yeah – me, the one who can't cook! Is going OK so far tho… have fried the onions, garlic, mushrooms and pepper, and am mulling over the rest of Abby's detailed instructions. (Oh, am making her famous lasagne.)

She dropped recipe by yesterday, along with the plate she'd made for O… a rather groovy one with '21' in the middle (his grand old age) and some funky patterns and things around the edge… He loves it… says it's his best pressie yet, but that's only coz I haven't given him MINE yet (am giving it to him at the meal this eve). HATE to say it, but she's so good at those plates… look just like they've come straight from the shelves of Whittards, but better! Will I make plates like that when me and O are married with kids? Hmm. Not sure am talented enuf. Anyway, enuf of plates, must get back to the meal prep… will keep you informed!

7:31 pm Is going tres tres bon! Am top French chef in classy French restaurant! Errrr… no, swipe that… lasagne's Italian, innit? Am top ITALIAN chef then! Hurrah pour moi! (Sorry, no grasp of Italian language whatsoever.)

Have added mince to frying onions etc… is lookin yummy already. Abby says to add spinach at this point, but will leave out… Tastes great in hers, but is bound to be total disaster in mine. Cheese sauce is done… and is even thick, like it's supposed to be! Didn't realise I was such a natural at this cooking malarky… ought to become famous Cn chef.

Ooohhh… gap in the market… Cn celebrity chef… Don't think there is one! Could go on tour with Jamie…

'Jude and Jamie!'

Nope, would have to be:

'Judith Singleton and Jamie Oliver'

as then we've got same no of syllables in our names – gotta be a winning combination! We could do the Good Food Show… and Greenbelt/ S Harvest etc! I could be his sidekick… or would he be mine? Sure his good lady wife Jules wouldn't mind… she and O could keep each other company, while Jamie and I battle off the swarms of fans! Sorted. Right, back to work…

7:46 pm Not sure that my schedule is really working, as the lasagne is not technically in oven yet. Is not technically finished yet anyway, and oven only technically switched on a few mins ago… whoopsie whoo! No probs, perhaps I'll do the 'Flopsy' thing before the meal, to distract from the fact that meal massively late.

Cheese sauce not doing too well. It was fine, but have just realised that, in my excitement, I didn't (technically) put any cheese in it. Found some at back of my shelf on fridge... poss a little old, as had certain amount of mould growing on one side, but seemed fine when I chopped this bit off. Added to sauce and reheated... but now it's all runny... baaahhhh!

Mince got just a TAD burnt, in that I answered phone (Libs) and got distracted for a bit. (Abby's instructions say to keep an eye on mince, but we can't all be Little Miss Perfect now, CAN we?) Am here on my tod, btw... everyone kindly cleared out for the eve, so me and O could enjoy the eve alone together... Bless.

OK, am going to be brave, and put burnt mince and runny sauce (avec mouldy cheese) together, with some sheets of lasagne, and cook it, in the hope that it will magically morph into what I eat at my sister's oh-so-often!

Huh... Recipes... who needs 'em?

8:31 pm Me, I need them. Or at least I need the v specific one, in my sister's own meticulous handwriting, that I threw in the bin, a while back, when I was getting all hot n bothered n annoyed with it, and myself, for not making a decent lasagne. Main prob was, I put lasagne in, at 190 degrees, as per recipe... but didn't take note of how long it was supposed to stay in. And SINCE chucking recipe in bin, I've had a bit of a clear-up, and chucked a whole lot of other stuff in bin... thus I greeted O at door with...

'Pleeeeeeeeease stop me from screaming... pleeeeeeeeease rescue the recipe from the bin... I just can't FACE IT!!!'

And retrieve it he did... he's fab like that. As I watched him roll up his sleeves, and plunge his arm courageously into the minging pile of mingness... I wondered if Jamie ever had to get Jules to do this... or would his cameraman rise to the occasion? Not sure about touring with Jamie now. Esp as 'saved' recipe said it should have been in for ½ hour, but after only ¼ it looked well-burnt on top, even tho twas pretty cold in the middle! O said that might have been coz I put it in when oven not hot enuf... smashin'.

Never mind, we're gonna heat up the pasties in the microwave (the ones O brought with him... 'just in case!'). He's just sorting them out now... thus my opportunity to pop up here and keep you informed. WHY do I do this,

Bob? WHY do I tell you everything? I am odd!

9:51 pm The evening is over. O has gone home. WHY so early? Coz we're done. Me n him. Over. Finito. Ended. Laid to rest.

Am in a daze... an amazing sense of day jar vous (must learn how to spell that properly).

After we'd had our pasties, we settled on sofa, with MTV as backround music, and chatted, and errr... kissed, and other stuff. We've been a lot more careful recently, re the whole 'touching' thing. Generally, it's not too much of a prob – I assume coz we're aware of it now. Haven't really given it much thought of late. Tonight was a bit serious tho... O got a bit 'involved', to the extent where it was ME who had to pull away, and not him. He then went over to sit on chair opposite. I suddenly remembered that I'd not got round to giving him his rabbits and said I had to go get his pressie... when he said:

'Jude, I hate to say this, again... but I think we really should think about calling it a day. Don't get me wrong - I love you so much, but it's not feeling like the right thing for me, for us... not the right timing, not God's timing... what do you think?'

What did I think? That I wanted him to stop saying such things, and let me get his rabbits. But I just asked him to explain what he meant, and sat back, feeling the pain whoosh thru me instantly, and the tears niggling behind my eyes, queuing up to get out. He started talking, while I went into 'dentist' mode. What was it Mum had advised me to do, that worked so well to distract myself from the pain? Relax... imagine all body parts relaxing, one by one... focus on happy things... don't let the...

'JUDE! I know you well enough by now to know when you're not LISTENING to me... this is important!'

So much for that then. Listen I did. Yeah, was all about timing really. He wanted me to know how much he loved me, and loved being with me, and had kinda pictured us being together, long-term... but how recently he wasn't sure it was best for us, and what God wanted for us. We both need to get on with our study, and we prob spend too much time together to get the grade we deserve. We both need to spend more time working out things with God.

Couldn't help think that both these things were more about ME than him. He's doing fine with his study, but I'm heading for failure unless things change soon. He seems all sorted with God – it's me who's having weird dreams and wanting to book a one-way ticket to Africa, and doesn't know what God's saying to me about my life and my future.

In the words of that well-known song (well, sorta):

'It's all about me … and all this is for me … it's not about you …'

Would've sung it to O, if the occasion allowed, but it didn't. Was he doing this for my benefit then? Perhaps. He seemed sincere tho. He is painfully honest – I believe every word.

I really thought he was 'the one'… but how can he be, if he doesn't want to be with me any more? Huh?

So here I sit, in my room, staring at the card thingy I never got to give him, with Flopsy and Mopsy looking up at me, wondering why they never got to do their job. Well, guess they are doing their job, as already paid for etc… but so wanted O to know about it…

Am also lookin at pile of Oscar's sex books, that I've just KICKED over, so they're all over the floor. That was another thing that was bothering O… our little 'heavy petting' issue. Hmm. Sex. Who needs it? Wish it didn't exist. It's spoilt the best thing I ever had… and we didn't even DO it.

Baaaah. Can hear some of the others coming back… will have to act all 'normal' for a bit… calmly tell them I've split up with O… then rush back up here for long sob into pillow…

Mon 17 Oct

Why is life so complicated? Just had some Coco Pops with Neil and Gaz. They're always the last of housemates to come down to the kitchen in the am… They claim it's coz they have the furthest to come (top floor), but hardly think it can take them an hour to walk down that one extra flight of stairs!

Anyway, whilst stuffing C Pops into gob, read the label on milk carton (just to pass the time… anything to stop me thinking about me and O)…
'Whole fresh pasteurised homogenised standardised less than 4% fat MILK'
Why can't it just say: 'MILK'?

Life would be so much better if you knew what you were doing with it, if I knew what I was doing with it. Does God have any sort of plan for me, or has he run out of good plans… and am left with a naf one from the dregs pile, that involves studying milk labels?

Milk incident almost made me cry. Am depressed re the whole thing… but somehow I think the right decision has been made. I think. Has it? Hmm.

Post-BURP O was there. Had ½ wondered if he'd give it a miss, so we wouldn't have to see each other, rather like before, but it doesn't seem to be like that this time round. There was no awkwardness when we saw each other. Essentially, apart from no physical contact… it was not that different from when we were going out. He asked me about my day and if I was OK, and I asked him about his and if he was OK, and it turned out that we were both a bit down, but mainly OK, and feeling it's all for the best.

How civil.

More to the point…

How final.

Is so obvious that we're thru now. Guess will have to live with just being his mate, but is that what I want?

Arrrrggghhhh!! I don't even know what I want! How can I have what I want if I don't even KNOW what I want?

Does God really have a 'chosen one' for us all, to spend the rest of our lives with? If you DON'T marry the person God wanted you to, does that mean that the person THEY were SUPPOSED to marry is then without a person to marry, or does God then do 'swapsies' and re-allocate the bereft person a new mate? Is all too complicated… not sure if can even be bothered to ask such questions anymore, let alone try to figure out the answers.

Oh, Bible study was well good… On 'holistic mission', like Mike had mentioned the other day. The bloke leading it was really spot on. Gave me TONS more to think about… For example, he said that we are called to care for the poor and oppressed in the world, but that this can mean so many things… There are people in our country (in this uni even) who are oppressed, and need our support, love etc. Our country also has its fair share of people who are poor… perhaps not quite as poor as those in the 3rd World, but v much at the bottom of the pile and v depressed with it, living in this rich Western World, that says you have to keep up with everyone else.

He said stuff about loneliness, which made me think of Maisie. O and I gave each other a knowing look, right at the same time.

The verse he went on and on about was the one where Jesus says he came that we could have life, life in all its fullness.

This is what we are here for: to help others have a fullness of life, to have caring relationships with others... to have a rel with God.

I really paid attention when he talked about suffering... some of what he said made me wanna puke, re people suffering due to famine or war or persecution etc. Lost him for a few mins tho, when my dream floated thru my head again... I looked at her more closely than before... what was her actual problem... hunger/pain/loneliness/loss of child/fear/not knowing God... perhaps a mixture of these. Did she live in Africa, or in a rundown council flat in London somewhere? Whatever the answer, I knew that NOW I had a mission – to sort people out! To help the people God wanted me to, put them and him 1st, and me 2nd... That must be it, I think.

He ended by saying that the reason he talked about 'holistic' mission was that it meant the whole person was taken into account – physically, mentally, emotionally, spiritually etc.

He said the vastness of the challenge shouldn't put us off... If we're willing, God will help us help others. We ended in prayer... the best prayer time have had in ages... really thanked God for what had been said, and for answering my questions re the dream and what I had to do about it. Found myself adding to my silent prayer a quick request for O and me to get back together, but then just added that it was up to him. Not sure I want it to be up to him really, but it seemed the right thing to say.

Tons of people came back to ours to watch the next musical, carefully selected by our expert, Jon:

The Sound of Music!

Was v fab. Lots of karaoke-style singing along. Julie Andrews rocks! Fax informed us all that it's actually based on a true story, and that the real 'Maria' had a cameo role in the film, but she's only in the distance for about 10 secs and you can't even make out her face properly! Poor love.

Musicals really leave you on a high... they always turn out so hunky-dory! Despite my current situation, couldn't help but feel quite hyped afterwards.

Just as credits were rolling, who should stroll in but Reuben! Saw a few slightly iffy looks thrown his way... guess some of us thought he'd come to plug Nazarene's next gig...

And a gig he did plug:

HIS BAPTISM!!

Yeah, he said he'd drifted so far off he was almost gone altogether... but has been chatting more and more with God (and Mike) recently, and has got himself sorted (well, God's got him sorted). He wants to make it public and booked his baptism (2 weeks this Sun) to do so! We are all well-chuffed... He seems genuine too... he's given up Nazarene!

Wow! V odd to have him back again... he squeezed in on the sofa, next to O, meaning I had a good view of the 2 of them... the bloke I obsessed about for months and the bloke I'm obsessing about now.

A pair of obsess-ees.

Barbie plasters

Tue 18 Oct

Everyone is being v nice to me re my return to the world of Singleton-ness. Everyone that is, apart from my own MOTHER.

Rang her today to let her know (interrupted their game of Uno...'The Grand Final'... what have I started?!). I know I didn't tell them last time, but this is looking to be more... concrete, so thought they ought to know, like.

'Disappointed' would not be the word to use... try 'mortified' or 'suicidal'... Was as if I'd blown my one and only chance to bag a bloke (I haven't, have I? Please say no!).

They were both CRAZY over O... a bit like the son they never had, or whatever. Perhaps she prefers him to me. Charming! Is like I've failed them, and entire human race. What does she know anyway? A bit of support and TLC would've been great. Thx for nothing, Mum. She really does have NO idea at all how I'm feeling.
None.
Baahh.

Had a better phone call just now, that made up for the pants one with Mum... Reuben has asked me to do the Bible reading at his baptism... said I can even choose the passage! How cool is that! Never been asked to do that at a baptism before = v cool.

Wed 19 Oct

Got email from Mum this am apologising for how she might have come across yesterday, saying she DID understand what I was going thru, and attatching a poem, that SHE wrote, when she was my age, at Bible college, and had just finished with a bloke...

Where your heart is...

Father, this restless heart too strongly yearns
For treasure which the world can give –

For friendship, understanding, love and care,
Another heart, my heart and thoughts to share,
For singing brooks, fresh fields and mountain air,
For rest from toil, in calm and peace to live.

Father, these restless hands too quickly turn
To clutch and grasp at every seeming gain –
At sure position, friends and being known,
Honour and influence, a Christian home,
Never while life shall last to feel alone,
After desert thirst, fresh springtime rain.

So father, take these hands, this heart.
Thine is earth's store to give or keep from me.
And if such treasure I should not receive,
Nought from the world to take, instead to give,
It is enough – but let me live with thee live:
My treasure is with thee.

Had to skip a lecture so could stay here and cry and cry and cry (but in a good way). So she DID understand. She HAS been here. Who'd have thought! Always weird to think your parents were young once, esp someone like Mum. Bless.

Thur 20 Oct

9:51 am

Ouch-a-rooney! Just given myself the billionth paper cut this month... paper should be banned, or assignments – one or the other. Was complaining about paper cuts during boring bits of *The Sound of Music* (come on... it's not ALL fab) but no one seemed at all interested. Trif.

4:18 pm Could O have accessed these letters somehow... sneaked into my room when I was out earlier, and read this am's comment? Doubt it, but oddly enuf, when I got back from town, there was a packet of Barbie plasters outside my bedroom door, with an attached scribbled note...

For all those paper cuts!

How cool is that?! He has remembered how cute I thought those W the Pooh tissues were, and has done it again, but with plasters! What does this mean... that he wants to get back together... that he's just a concerned friend... What?!

Won't go OTT by ringing him now... will wait till I next see him... Need to play it cool, in case this is my final chance to get my life back again.

Have put 3 plasters over the worst cuts... they stand out big-time – feel like singing 'I'm a barbie girl, in a barbie wo-o-orld'... but won't.

Off to work now – hope they appreciate my new fashion statement... straight off the catwalk of Mothercare!

Fri 21 Oct

11:01 pm

Can't help but notice that I am not ½ as depressed as I was the last time this happened... is this coz I don't feel the same way about O, or just coz I've gone past thinking I can do anything to change what's happened. Is acceptance the same as 'giving up'?

Got all that 'holistic mission' stuff on my mind most of the time... Reading the Bible a whole lot more, to understand it all... well, some of it anyway. Still trying to find an appropriate passage to read out at R's baptism... not sure the widows and orphans bit really fits the occasion, dynamic as it is!

Another passage I've been mulling over is

Ahh, door... think am the only resident here at present... must go answer it... wonder if it's O?

Post-door answering Hmm. Was Reuben. Well, IS Reuben, as he is downstairs watching *This Morning* while I am (supposedly) getting ready to go into town with him. He called round...

TO ASK IF I LIKED THE PLASTERS!!!

They were from him. Him. Not O.

He says he needs a new 'funky version' Bible and that I might be of use to him in picking out a good one.
Fine.
That's fine.
That's what pals do, isn't it... help each other with their shopping? Quite normal. In no way could it be described as a 'date'. We're just 2 BURPers popping to Bymouth Cn bookshop in search of a Bible. Sorted. Hope we don't bump into O tho. Don't want him to think it's anything MORE than a

quick shopping trip, which it isn't.

Is it?

Hmmmmmmmmm...

Post-Bible shopping Our little 'pop' to the shops lasted a whole 4 hours!

We spent ages browsing the Bibles, and eventually we choose *The Message*. Not really a 'version', I'm told, but is useful to read all the same. Makes a lot of stuff leap off the page at you, and that's gotta be good. Then he suggested we grab something to eat at W Spoons... he was paying... who am I to turn down free food!?

Have to admit, despite how annoying he's been of late – now he's done his prodigal son bit and made up with God – he's quite good to talk to. We spent a long time comparing our past experiences, comparing my 'doubt' to his 'rebellion'. He says what he did is much worse, as he KNEW God was real, but choose not to stick with him, preferring to do his own thing (which mainly seems to have involved the band, beer and gals... funnily enuf. Hmm... guess these things were his 'idols' then – poor deluded chap!). He's dead keen now tho... wants to focus on God, get his life sorted, get 'a vision' re what God has in store for his future etc etc. Is way ahead of me. I did my prodigal daughter bit at Easter... and am STILL pretty confused!

R is dead funny... my meal (one of those posh hot salad thingies) went cold in the end, due to so many chuckle-filled interruptions whilst eating. I spotted a fresher/BURPer working behind the bar. Told R she goes to the local Pentecostal church. He replied:

'Right, well I'll give her our pudding order in tongues then and she can interpret it... It'll be good practice for her.'

Not sure if this is blasphemous or something... but caused me to spit a lot of tiny bits of sun dried tomato in his face (due to laughing)... He didn't seem to mind.

Now I'm reflecting on my time with R, am starting to feel a tad confused again... Am I supposed to be with him? Is he 'the one'? Was it just that I had to wait for him to come back to God? Was being with O all a mistake, which is why it's now over, so I can be with who I'm supposed to be with?

I still fancy R, naturally. But I don't KNOW him v well... we're not close, like me and O. I love O. I don't LOVE R. But could I? Am I supposed to work on this/allow it to happen? Is he even interested in me anyway?

C'mon God... TELL ME TELL ME TELL ME TELL ME TELL ME TELL ME!

Not going out this eve... feels like a Ben-n-Jerry's-(Phish Food flave)-in-front-of-*Holby-City* eve to me... kinda down, tho will pull thru soon (I think).

Sat 22 Oct

Just woke up. Feeling fat, due to far too much Phish Food last night.

Also feeling totally PANTS. Not sure I WILL pull thru, now have given more thought. Is all v well for God to show me all this stuff re helping others who are suffering, etc... but what about my personal life? My b/f, and lack thereof? Shall I just give up and remain single (yikes!) or beg O to have me back, or give consideration to Reuben... or what?

Need to talk with someone who knows this sort of thing... Mike's good at sorting people out... will ring him at home right now...

He's not there. No one answered. Huh. Where's your uni chaplain when you want him. Thought he's supposed to 'be there' for us and all. Not a v good start when he's not even IN. Will try his mobile...

Got answerphone message. Trif. Super. What if I had an emergency and needed him to... wait! This IS an emergency... I need to know what to do with my life... if THAT'S not an emergency then I dunno what is. Will try his office at the church...

Can see a bit of a pattern forming. Not there. Answerphone.

What kind of a chaplain is he? Does he do this to everyone who needs his help, or does he just save this kinda treatment for me?

Arrrrgggghhhhh! Baaaah! Sorry, know this sounds 'off', but REALLY angry with him now... not sure I wanna get his advice after all... perhaps he just pretends to be concerned for us all, but in actual fact... couldn't give a damn.

Not going to BURP outreach thing tonight... can't face it. Don't feel like telling others to follow a God that doesn't tell you what to do re relationships. Sound petty? Well tough – is just the way I feel.

Sun 23 Oct

Considered going to Mike's church this am, just so could see him after service, and chat. Yeah, know I said I didn't want to speak to him... but

REALLY have to speak with someone or am going to explode. Don't think any of my mates are particularly qualified to advise me, really. Don't want any of them to know what a big fat loser I am, either.

Backed out of going to Mike's church at last minute... Not on my own, would feel a right lemon. Ended up not going to my church either, but popping to Tesco for another couple of tubs of Ben & Jerry's (one Phish Food and one Karamel Sutra, which reminded me that REALLY must return Oscar's sex books... or perhaps could just get away with dumping them in library or something... or in nearest SKIP perhaps).

So, it's just been me, my ice cream and the telly (inc E *Enders* omnibus) so far today... what incredible fun. Sometimes, I wish that...

Bah. Phone. Wonder if it's O...

Nope. Was Mike. He was just settling down to read the paper, when he felt he should give me a ring... He hoped I could tell him why! Told him. Was quite honest... told him how pee-ed off I was that he wasn't 'there' for me. Was in that kind of in-yer-face mood. He listened to every word, then proceeded to inform me that Sat is his day off. It's his 'family day'... they were spending the day with friends. Errrrrr.... whoops! How was I supposed to know he had a day off... he never mentioned it before!

Guess I don't really think of him as having a life, outside of sorting us lot out!

He was fine about it tho. Said he was off out again in a bit, but that I was welcome to come over and chat with Jane, if I wanted. I did want, badly.

Feel real guilty about what I said to Mike, about being so angry that he wasn't 'on call' 24/7. He must work far more hours than he's required to.

Post-Jane Jane is so cool. Not nec cool as in 'trendy', but just so sorted, content... knows what she's doing with her life etc. Perhaps I ought to find myself an ace chaplain to marry... it seems to do the trick!

Anyway, she really helped. BEFORE the kettle had even boiled, I was in tears... saying how I didn't know what was going on in my life, and how I was such a PANTS Cn and might as well give up coz my life is going nowhere.

She said stuff about about us not having idols, and how, perhaps, my obsessing about having a b/f was an idol in my life – one I had to get rid of, so I could put God 1st. Was a bit annoyed at 1st... thought she was being a bit OTT, but then thought back to all that stuff on 'idols' and suchlike that's been floating in n out of my head for a while... perhaps she has a point.

Perhaps.

By the time my coffee was placed on kitchen table in front of me, I was crying even more, complaining that now I knew I really WAS pants at being a Cn, and had even more reason to give up. What would God want with me now, anyway? Have been obsessing re blokes all my life (well, ever since I can remember)... How CAN I change? It's just part of who I am, innit?

Instead of saying something useful (which I was kinda fishing for at this point) Jane went to kitchen drawer and got out some string. She then climbed on kitchen table, reached up to ceiling, and sellotaped one end of string to it, allowing the rest of the string to dangle down to touch the table. Without a word, she got a handful of pegs from the washing basket on the table (I'd obviously arrived mid hanging-of-washing-on-line). She put them in front of me, and then said:

'Right, Jude, if God is right up there on the ceiling... where is... errrr... Mother Teresa?'

and handed me a peg.

Hmm... OK, not too hard... fairly near to God, but not right on ceiling, obviously... opted for peg to go about ½ m from ceiling.

Then I had to do the following: Billy Graham, Matt Redman, Nicky Gumbel... followed by...

a gossip, a liar, a thief, a murderer and a rapist.

So, before I'd even started my coffee, I was staring at a dangling piece of string, with 9 pegs dotted up and down it... some nearer to God, and some nearer to the table. So far, so simple.

Sat back and started 1st slurp of much-needed coffee, when she leaped in with...

'And now you, Jude... where are you?'

Ahhh. Not so simple. Like, am hardly down there with the murderers... but I have been known to gossip, and lie... but can't poss be up with the likes of the Cn celebs... think Jude think... must be a right place to put my peg... errrr... done.

Put it kinda just between the 'gossip' and 'liar' pegs... at least she'll think I'm tres humble, if nowt else!

Sat back again, to view my position on the string... hmm... quite a long way from God then... figures... is just how I feel. Jane wasn't saying anything. Got involved with my coffee again... how hard can it be to actually DRINK the thing?

Jack then darted into kitchen, in only a way a 4-year-old boy can 'dart'... asking for a biscuit, and a drink, and to have the TV channel changed over... all in one breath. Mum replied in the affirmative, but only on condition that he pull the string down from the ceiling. A slightly confused but obedient child willingly did the deed. Whooomph! It fell down, caught the edge of the table... then landed in a heap on the floor.

'There,' she said. 'That's where all our pegs really are... whoever we are, whatever we've done, whatever we're gonna do... it's in the Bible, Jude... we're all 100% FAILURES as far as God's concerned. Sinners. Selfish sinners. Self-obsessed selfish sinners!

'That's why Jesus made that sacrifice... remember?

'So we could be God's friends, despite our pathetic selves. You're right, you are pathetic, but so am I, so's Mike... We all are. But, coz of Jesus, we don't have to get hung up about it!

'Of course we should try to be like him... or rather, allow him to change us... but it's a process, Jude... we'll never be right up there on the ceiling till we go to heaven.... till we get home. Comprendez vous?'

Yeah, I did comprendez, pretty much... and even got to drink my coffee in the end, even tho it had gone a tad cold. When Jack was all seen to, and settled back in the lounge (Ribena/2 jaffa cakes/*Tweenies*), Jane added that I ought to concentrate on my rel with God, put him 1st... and not worry myself about everything else. After all, even helping the poor and needy is only 'humanitarian aid' if it doesn't spring from knowing God and his love for us all.

Was a lot to take in... have been back here for hours now, but it's still all a bit of a whir in my head. Feel like I OUGHT to have it all sussed now, but haven't. Am better off than I was *before* talking with her (and demo with pegs!), but still not quite right.

From what she said, the bit that keeps cropping up in my head is about none of us ever being perfect until we 'go home'. Never really thought of it in that way before. The idea of heaven is kinda distant and 'odd'.

But 'home'... that's good.

That sounds good.

Mon 24 Oct

Really am getting behind with revision/assignments at the mo... got so much on my mind. Tend to start off listening to lecturer, trying to take it all in... but then drift off into my own little world, trying to sort my head out etc.

Today Prof Carr had to compete with the following:

1| *Does my obsession with having a b/f REALLY count as an idol that gets in the way of my rel with God?*
2| *If so, does that mean I ought to chuck in the idea of having a b/f?*
3| *If not, will O ever take me back?*
4| *Ought I to consider starting something with Reuben?*

And so on.

Sas' bloke was our 'guest' who did BURP Bible study. Quite basic... all about God's love for us, despite our sin etc (made me think of the pegs hanging from ceiling!). Whispered to Libs at the end that it was hard not to stare at his nice bum... she kinda smiled, but looked deep in thought. So went off to consult Lydia on the issue and she said I shouldn't be checking out blokes' bums, as it was lust... but then she smiled and said that she totally agreed. Ho ho!

All back here afterwards, for... you guessed it... another musical!
Summer Holiday, with Cliff Richard and co.

Was fab. Couldn't have squeezed anyone else in our lounge if you tried. Even Gaz was there... as bored in his room on his own... he even managed to cut down his use of the 'f' word, slightly. The 'f' word doesn't really fit with *Summer Holiday*... trust me!

Just like with the other Mon eve sessions... felt SO good when it was over! They make me feel so good, ready to burst into song at the next appropriate moment! Guess is coz it's all a dream-world, where everything turns out OK in the end... the boy gets the gal, everyone lives happily ever after etc.

Hmm... what would be MY 'happily ever after'?
In my musical (errr... soundtrack yet to be added) we've had the 'gal meets boy no 1' thing, that then doesn't work out, but then does, but then doesn't... and then 'boy no 2' comes on the scene...

So what's the ending?

1] Gal gets back with boy no 1 and lives happily ever after?

2] Gal gets together with boy no 2 and lives happily ever after?

3] Gal gets neither of them, falls into depression, leaves uni, lives on the streets selling Big Issue?

Last option doesn't sound like the making of a blockbusting musical... but then whose life does, eh?

1:21 am Lots of noise coming from Gaz's room... not the real slim shady tho... Gaz, singing,

'3 days till our hol-i-day... 2 days till our hol-i-day... 1 more day, YES, 1 more day...' etc.

(Sorry, Bob – if you don't know the song, you'll have to go watch the film!) Not an 'f' word to be heard. Bless. Think living in a houseful of Cns is affecting him. If nothing else, he has been taught to appreciate Cliff Richard!

Phhwooooaarrrr! Cliff. Quite fancy him (in the film, not now, obviously).

O and R both there this eve, for BURP and musical. Chatted with them both, a bit... nothing worth reporting back tho. R is back on the committee now, as evangelism secretary. O was pretty quiet.

Wed 26 Oct

Been to visit Pete this am.

O mentioned last night that Mike was going to the prison today for a mtg with the chaplain there (or whatever) and, if I got a lift with him, I could visit Pete, which O was keen on me doing as he is well busy with study and won't be seeing him this week. Is nice that O feels I am still someone he wants to be involved in Pete's life... wish it meant spending time with him tho, not just his Dad.

Still, had good chat with Pete. He said that O is particularly stressed right now, which came as bit of a shock pour moi. Is all down to O's mum – she's steadily getting worse... Dr says she's not really capable of living on her own any more – needs to go into a home of some sort, or one of those flats where there's a warden to keep an eye on her, where old people live, or whatever.

Pete says O is gutted, feels guilty that he's not been there for her since he left home for uni... almost feels he ought to give up and go look after her.

Pete says he's told him he must do what he feels is right, but that he would be gutted if O left uni now. At the same time, Pete knows that his wife is in the state she's in coz of what he did to her… He doesn't really feel like he can advise O either way. Pete also said a lot of stuff about how guilty he still feels. Sort of managed to tell him about the pegs hanging from the ceiling thing… not sure I got it all right (where's Jane when you need her?!), but he seemed interested. Wish he would be a Cn again.

So is the reason O pulled the plug on me… coz he's stressing re family issues? If so, why didn't he just say that? Wouldn't it be best if we were together, so I could support him?

Will distract myself from browsing thru the bridal mag that Lauren's lent me… I am picking out the style of b'maid dress I want! Can't wait. Is gonna be so cool. OK, so would rather be Lauren (not preggie, but marrying the bloke I love), but being b'maid is almost as good… at least get to wear fab dress and get lots of attention… Must lose weight… but Ben & Jerry's is so scrumptious, is so hard!

Thur 27 Oct

Soooooooo didn't feel up to going to work this eve… fed up with it really. OK, so desperately need the money (the state of my bank account? Bob, don't even GO there!), but work seems so pointless. Don't particularly enjoy it. Count down the hours till it's all over and I can go home and crash. Still, work is work. MUST study harder, get degree, and get good job, that doesn't involve working such pants hours, and having to step over sick to collect glasses left in the far corners of the men's loos etc.

Libs was behind bar for most of the eve… this oldish (30?) bloke wouldn't leave her alone… clearly hoped for a bit of action. She ignored him most of the time, but just before closing time they seemed deep in convo. I left when she did, as owner was locking up for night. Old bloke still was on her arm! They giggled for the entire walk home (he'd been knocking back a fair few Stellas) while I just tried to look unphased. They left me outside my house, and headed for hers (a few streets away). Can't help but wonder if he's gonna spend the night with her.

Can't believe she could do this to Fax! He'll be gutted. What could he possibly have done to deserve this? Nowt, I guess. Is just Libs going back to her old ways, if she ever really left them in the 1st place. Perhaps Fax shouldn't have started something with her before she became a Cn. Don't think she ever WILL be one, however interested she is. Sound pessimistic? Sorry. Sure am right tho.

Am gonna ring her to find out what she's up to… perhaps am jumping to conclusions…

No, my jumping was dead accurate. It was 'him' in the background, nagging her to get back into bed, that gave me the biggest clue. She tried to 'shussh' him, but the damage had been done.

Right, am going to tell Fax…

No, course I'm not. That would be interfering. But hate to think of him not knowing his g/f is messing around behind his back.

Fri 28 Oct

They've split up.
Duncs n Lauren.

Can't believe it. Lauren's gone back to her parents for the weekend, and is all in a state, apparently. Duncs says their getting married was all for the wrong reasons. It was just coz of the baby – they felt they HAD to, when marriage shouldn't be like that. He added that they didn't really argue about it, but talked it thru, over and over, and decided to cancel the wedding. He still plans to be the supportive father, and they'll be good friends, but not hubbie and wife. She's gonna live at home, and perhaps resume her degree later on in life (she was quitting her degree anyway, but her and Duncs were going to rent a house in Bymouth so Duncs could stay at uni).

Have NO idea what to say re whole thing. They must know what they're doing, I guess. Wish they didn't have to go thru all this. Will ring Lauren this eve, check she's OK.

I won't be bridesmaid after all. Shame.
Looks like I'm not the only one who's destined never to be married then.

7:35 pm Have given this a lot of thought, and am gonna ring him. Yep. I know am doing the right thing and no one's gonna stop me…
He didn't react in quite the way I expected. Fax said he was v 'disappointed' that Libs had a bloke to stay the night, but that it was her decision to do so.

How calm can you get?! He asked me to continue to pray for her. Will do so now...

Done. Rang Libs also, but phone switched off. Hmm.

Mon 31 Oct

8:49 am

Aarrrrgghhhh! R just rang... to ask if I wanted to go for a drink with him this eve after BURP. He mumbled something about wanting a viable excuse not to go to a Halloween party that all his housemates were pressing him to go to (so glad I live with mainly Cns). Kind of reminded him that we usually come back to my place after BURP, for our weekly doseage of 'musical'. He kinda went 'Oh, of course... yeah,' and said he'd see me there.

Gaz has been hyper all am... can't decide if he's gonna be a ghost, something from Harry Potter... or go in drag as 'Satan's sister'... to the Halloween party this eve. Keeps coming down from his room with different outfits, expecting me to be the judge of which is best. Not easy, when all you WANNA say is that you don't really go in for Halloween seeing as is all evil and anti-God etc. Is being quite picky re what to wear, for a bloke, anyway. Satan's sis is clearly the most effective outfit so far (is v v freakily scary, esp with the horns and pitchfork). Each time he comes down to parade in front of me in the lounge, he says I ought to 'loosen up' and come to the party too. Silly boy. Still, is nice to be wanted... 1st R, and now Gaz/Satan's freaky sister.

Wish O wanted me. I want him.

Oh no, now that's set me off. Need to have pause typing to cry...

Quite a big pause really (½ hour). Kept thinking I was OK, but then something teeny would set me off crying again, like thinking back to stuff we used to do together, and to all the plans I had dreamed about for our future. Bah!

7:16 pm Was just setting off to go to BURP, when realised I really didn't wanna. The v thought of seeing O, and having to be all 'normal' around him when all I wanna do is have a massive hug, is total nightmare. Also don't want R asking me to pub again, and O hearing. If O's as down as his dad says, it might upset him all the more. Still, I've got my life to live. That drink with R is quite appealing. He does make me laugh, and we've sure got lots in common.

Nope… will stay here and get down to some study. Soon. Just after *Holby City*.

8:38 pm Getting a bit freaked out as BURPers will be here soon, to watch musical… How can I avoid them – go to bed? At this hour? They'll never fall for it. Or, I could… hang on… door…

Satan's sister. Asking one last time if I wanted to come, as he's off now. Have said yes. Don't freak, Bob. Is not as if I'm dressing up or anything. Like Gaz says, it's only a party with a theme… is not as if they'll be doing tarot cards or anything. Harmless bit of fun. He's calling for me again in 5 mins, so must be speedy-gon-Jude-ez and get ready!

Post H'ween party Hmm. Interesting evening. Can't tell you a lot re the party, as only there for about 10 mins. Gaz was v chatty and nice on way there, but deserted me as soon as we got to the party (S Union bar). Trif. Some people had really gone to town on their costumes – must have hired them out or something. Felt a little underdressed in my jeans and hoodie. Gaz was right about one thing tho – was just a party… booze, flirting, snogging, dancing… maybe even some drugs going on somewhere (but they'd be lucky not to get banned from the Union). Same old same old.

Spotted some people from my course, dressed as a group of aliens (what is the collective name for aliens… A herd? A flock?). What aliens have got to do with Halloween is beyond me. They looked far too plastered to be worrying about the appropriateness of their costumes. So glad I don't drink anymore. Have got O to thank for that. Really didn't want to approach aliens – just wanted to get outta there, asap. It was something about the atmosphere: oppressive, freaky… aggressive almost.

Wanted, above all, to ring O, but couldn't as he was leading Bible study tonight, and might still be wrapping things up. Libs was working. Others would be at BURP and don't drive (or do drive but don't have car). Only person who was in a position to help me was R. Rang him, asked him if we could have that drink after all. Asked him to pick me up from SU bar. He started to say, 'Hang on, isn't that where the Halloween…' but I stopped him mid-sentence, and begged him not to let the others there at BURP know, as tres embarrassing for someone on committee to be doing this sort of thing. Bad witness to freshers and all that. He drove straight over and got me.

Spent rest of evening at quiet country pub, a few miles out of Bymouth. They didn't seem to have the foggiest idea that it was H'ween! Hurrah! We chatted till closing time... don't know where the 2 hours went, I really don't.

He *really* is hot. Can't deny it. Found my thoughts flipping between how much I was enjoying R's company, to how much I missed O and wanted him back, to how much R was making me laugh, to how much I respected and loved O, and so on and so on.

He dropped me off. Tried so so hard to sneak in past lounge, and dart up the stairs to my room, without anyone spotting me... but Lydia was just coming downstairs after a trip to loo... almost banged right into her I was going so fast! Had no choice but to join them all in lounge then. No one seemed too interested in why I wasn't at BURP, except for O, who asked if everything was OK. I replied that it was, and could he shussh up as I wanted to catch the end of *Oliver!*.

Good film. Great ending.
'As long as he needs me...'

Out with the wedding mags

Wed 2 Nov

Bumped into my tutor today, who was loitering in the corridor outside the lecture hall, just as we were all piling out. Tried to get away with giving her a quick smile, that included a subliminal 'Hey, it's great to see you, but I've got so much to do I really must get going' look.

She's obviously not v tuned into the subliminal tho... as she kinda stepped into my path and asked if we could have a quick word.

She's clearly not v up on her definitions either, as her 'quick' word ended up lasting ¾ hour! Basically, she said she's noticed how my marks have been steadily slipping, and, added to the results of my last lot of exams... I really needed to WORK a tad more. Without beating around the bush, she said that, if I didn't 'knuckle down' soon, I'd prob not pass my next exams, and would be O.U.T.

We (she) discussed coming up with a detailed timetable of revision, and attending special sessions on assignment research, preparation, execution, evaluation... etc. Made me want to carry out some execution on her... but, in all fairness, the woman's dead right.

Is all cool – just gotta motivate myself and get my act together... gotta gotta GOTTA!!!

Popped over to Lydia and Jon's for a bit. Was a bit down after encounter with Ms Tutor. They were concerned about my break-up with O, and wanted to know if I was coping OK. Told them that I was nowhere near coping OK, but that they weren't to panic... I'd sort myself out.

What a lie! I'm the last person who can sort me out.

They cheered me up tho, in that they fed me and let me 'coo' over their wedding piccies (for the billionth time!). They seem cool with their marriage now, which is fab.

Jon and I did have small disagreement tho... he says Häagen Dazs is much better than Ben & Jerry's. I say... WHAT PLANET are you on, dude?!

Still, each to their own. He's only a bloke – wot does he know anyway?

Admittedly, I do go for Häagen Dazs 'tiramisu' flave... might go out and buy some now tho, if Tesco have got it in stock... just to show there's no hard feelings between me and Jon.

Not that he'll know I've eaten it... unless I save the empty tub and show him sometime, as proof!

Still not sure which verse to read at R's baptism... want it to be encouraging, but not namby-pamby... will just have to wait till something presents itself.

Errr... that is to say, till God 'gives' me the right verse, to use the correct Cn terminology!

Fri 4 Nov

5:39 pm

Bizarre! Mobile just rang (interrupting N*eighbours*)... the caller said:

'Is this Jude?' I replied that it was. 'Right, well this is PC Stevens, ringing from Bymouth Police Station. We have your friend Oren here, who is very drunk, and needs collecting. If you could—'

Didn't hear the end of it, as hung up. Not letting the joker get away with it! Can't think quite who it could be tho... sounded a BIT like Reuben, but I can't think why he would do something like this. Wouldn't be anyone from BURP, surely. Might be Gaz... yeah, actually it MUST be as HIS surname is Stevens... and he knows perfectly well that O is my ex. Still, a rather cruel 'joke' if you ask me. He'll prob ring me back in a min to apologise and... ah, phone again...

Same thing again, but this time he went on to say that, if I couldn't collect him myself, then could I contact his next of kin etc. When Gaz had finished this alarmingly well-rehearsed speech, I confronted him with: 'C'mon Gaz... it's not big and it's not clever, so give it up mate.'

His reply:

'Errrr... right. I think you might have me confused with someone else. My name is PC Stevens, and I'm ringing from—'

I interrupted, but only coz it dawned on me that it really WAS a PC, and not just Gaz being annoying. Started to say that there must be some mistake as the Oren I knew didn't even drink. PC Stevens didn't appear too interested in his track record, just that O was with them now and the only thing that came out of him in a vaguely coherent fashion was my name and mobile no, so COULD I COME AND GET HIM?!

Must dash then…

Post-P Station Well, I've got a v v drunk O in my lounge. He's totally out of it, lying on the sofa (and continually falling on floor and needing to be put back on sofa) drifting between being unconscious, to ranting on about how someone needs to stop the sofa from moving, and his phone from ringing. Have just cleared up his 3rd lot of sick from carpet (not including the 2 times he was sick in Amos' car… I got Amos to collect O from police station as it's not far from where they live, and I wanna keep this whole thing quiet from the rest of BURP, if poss). What really bugs me is that I can just picture PC Stevens and his PC buddies, saying stuff like: 'Typical students… when will they learn?' etc. But it's not LIKE that at all. O doesn't even drink, usually. Who knows what this IS actually about tho. Amos says O was found 'causing a disturbance' in the High St, complete with an almost empty bottle of vodka. Freaky.

Oooh… phone again…

Was Pete. He said he's been trying to get thru to O, but he's not answering (ahh – this will explain why O's phone has been going off now and then… haven't dared answer it). Was well pleased with Pete's question: did I know if Mike knew much about 'Alpha for prisons' as his chaplain didn't seem to, but would be interested in running a course if he had the stuff. Pete says he wants to look again at the whole being a Christian thing. Wow! Excellent! Only odd thing was being able to hear O throwing up in the lounge whilst I listened to Pete in the safety of the kitchen. Didn't tell Pete about O, for obvious reasons… it'd break his heart for one thing.

There. Have actually arranged my duvet on the lounge floor now, so O can stay there, as he seems to like it there so much! Keep darting up here to my room for a few mins peace (and to write to you)… then am off downstairs again, to pick up bowl of hot soapy water and a flannel from kitchen… and start the clear-up-O process all over again. Is becoming like 2nd nature now, but in a bad way. HATE sick. Grim city.

He looks so ill… wish I could do more to help. The others will be back soon, so they'll have to know about him, but will plead for them to keep their traps shut re it. Hope they're fine with taking turns to sorting him out, as I am well-knackered.

Right, must ring Mike now, re Pete and that Alpha thingy…

Sat 5 Nov

5:04 am

Know it's well early, but have just been down to check on O (still on lounge floor). We've decided to leave him there, until he's able to move without throwing up. He seems OK… fast asleep. Lounge stinks of vomit… in fact, whole house does. Still, makes a change from poo. Am gonna try to get more sleep now, as kinda need it badly…

5:38 pm Am supposed to be getting ready for BURP outreach thingy, which is a bonfire/fireworks event that Fax has been sorting out all week. Haven't been v involved. Just can't see the point in going… not sure that being with other Cns, who know what their lives are about, will do me any good.

O left just after lunch. He wasn't 100%… Reuben drove him back to his place, and put him to bed. He's stopped being sick, which seems to be a good sign. He's been sleeping on and off all am, not being v talkative in-between times… bless 'im. Really wanna know what his drinking binge was all about, but will have to wait till he's ready to tell me, I guess. Is not like he's my b/f and I can demand some sort of explanation.

Poor O.

Forget the above… WILL go to BURP… will only be all lonely and depressed if spend the eve here, alone.

Post-bonfire A healthy turn-out, not that it meant much to me tho. What exactly are we all doing, huh? OK, so we kinda know God and all, but what's the purpose of our talking ABOUT him, if we're not really hearing FROM him. OK, if I'M not hearing from him. Had such a feeling of 'not belonging' that it really got to me. And, if I don't belong here, with these Cns, where do I belong… back at home? No way. Where then?

About 7 fireworks and 2 hotdogs in… I did a runner. Well, more of a jog really… was only 2 miles away from my place… couldn't get back quick enuf.

O wasn't at BURP… assumedly coz he's suffering with major hangover. Might just ring him now and see how he's doin…

Post-call He apologised a trillion times over. He made a point of saying that he's NOT turning out like his dad… it was just that everything got to him and he didn't know how to handle it… mainly re his mum and all that.

We had a good chat… prob the best one since we split up.

Wanted to ask if it was having all this on his mind that contributed to splitting up with me… but couldn't bring myself to… is not what he needs to hear right now, am sure.

As soon as our phone call was over, Reuben rang… checking I was OK, as he'd noticed I'd left early… Did I want him to come over?!

Said thx but no thx, as I needed early-ish night, after getting little sleep last night due to worrying about O down in the lounge. He seemed cool with that, and asked if I was still OK to do the Bible reading tomorrow… tried to remain cool as I said, 'Course, no worries,' when, in actual fact, I was freaking out as haven't chosen the passage yet, let alone practised reading it! Will go check it out now… don't feel like it tho… is not like the Bible is being of much use to me right now. OK, so I prob don't read it enuf. Hmm.

Not sure I feel as close to God as I have done, since we became pals again. Am blaming him for a lot of my pain, I guess. Huh.

Sun 6 Nov

8:38 am

There's 1½ hours to go, and still not sorted what I'm reading. Nothing seems right. Nothing makes sense. Sure it all made sense before, but now the words just swim in front of my eyes, boring me senseless. That's what I am – bored. In the fullest sense of the word… am bored with trying to sort my life/relationships out, am bored not hearing from God, am bored watching everyone else merrily tick along while I am so confused – am bored with the entire thing. Apathy… that's a better word for it I think. Not my fault tho… it's been induced by the situation I'm in, and my lack of power to change things. Ggggrrrrrrrrrrrr.

9:35 am Should be leaving soon, if gonna get a good seat. Sas has just shouted up that we're leaving in 2 mins. Don't think I'll go. Nothing for it but to fake headache or sim. Can't poss read out Bible bit (that I haven't found yet) in front of all those people, with conviction… when am so v lost.

10:04 am Did it. Fake headache thing didn't go down too well. They all begged me to come… but they had to go in the end, or they'd be late themselves. They'll all be there now, in the uni chapel. (Reuben wanted it there, instead of our normal church, as he wanted Mike to do it. No baptistry in chapel, so Mike's sorted out some sort of paddling pool thing, and is using a bucket of water!). Have asked Sas to do the reading. Kind of wish I was there now, but there you go. Wonder if O has made it? He said yesterday that he'd really try to, if he felt well enuf.

Hmm. Better get on with this assignment, I guess.

10:15 am Is no good... have got to go... if I go now, ought to be able to grab a bus that drops off somewhere near campus. Even tho I don't feel comfortable going, I just can't get away from the feeling that I OUGHT to be there... cheers, Bob...

11:31 pm OK, so I snuck in the back door, just as Sas was doing the reading:

'Jesus said ... I will come back and take you with me.'

BEFORE I'd even made it to a pew, my legs went all jelly-fied, and I started to cry... just like that. Sat down, holding onto the pew in front, for some kind of support. My head was down, the tears didn't stop. It was that verse... it was just what Jane had said about 'going home'. This is what hit me... that I wasn't supposed to feel 'at home' and all sorted whilst on earth... coz I WASN'T at home... and won't be till I die. Logic tells me (or perhaps it's God) that, the nearer I am to God while I AM on earth, the more at home I'll feel. He's coming back... to take me with him! Wow! Reminds me of Arnie Swartesknickers, in a film years ago, when he was protecting this lady from someone trying to kill her. He deposited her in a safe hiding place and told her to lie low and not move until he'd sorted her assassin out. Then he said, 'Then I'll come back and get you, OK?' And you knew he would, too. Totally reliable is old Arnie, as is God, my God.

Mike was preaching, but didn't catch much of it. Reminded me of the service in Romania, when I really 'felt' God, after such a massive dry patch. This was similar. I could really FEEL him. Not just think about him, pray to him or even reach out in desperation to him... but FEEL him... His presence, his personality, his love.

Thought back to how I'd 'found' God again in Romania. Thing is, it was also at this time I started going out with O. Got to admit it... have been soooooooooo obsessed with the whole b/f thing since then, that God hasn't really had much of a look in. 1st of all I was all plotting and scheming re how to 'keep' O, which took up a lot of my time... I even did more Cn-y things to impress him. Yikes.

All my prayers have revolved around O or having a b/f in general:

Lord, let O stay with me.
Lord, tell me if he's the one.
Lord, make me a better person so that O will like me more and want to stay with me.
Lord, why did he finish with me?
Lord, am I to get back with O, or is Reuben your chosen one for me?

And so on, and on, and on...

I must've related every chorus, Bible passage, sermon etc to ME and my need for a bloke. The only thing I've missed is getting to know God for WHO HE IS, and not what he can do for me.

Guess God's been TRYING to tell me stuff, esp re the suffering woman dream and all, and it has sunk in, but has always taken 2nd place to me and my b/f issues. How pathetic can you get? Don't answer that.

Sort of 'came round' to see Reuben, looking well happy, standing in a paddling pool that had material draped over it so it didn't look too much like it'd just come from Woolies. Mike held the bucket of water high, then poured it over R... the whole lot! We all cheered.

I felt such a peace. I felt peace and I felt God, or was it God that WAS the peace? Dunno.

As R went off to change, and 'It's all about you' started up... I realised that it really was now... all about him. I was also reminded of a line from that poem of Mum's:

So Father, take these hands, this heart.

Kept repeating it to myself, over and over. It felt like handing it all over to God, for good. Not just dumping it on him... just putting it in his care, so I could move on, move on with him.

Had my head practically in my lap, when felt tap on shoulder. Was Lauren, telling me they were going thru to hall for coffee n snacks. Looked up to see the church almost empty... I hadn't even been aware the service was over! I let her lead me to the hall, while I only had one thing on my mind: 'I will come back and take you with me' (John 14:3).

Reuben headed straight for me when we reached the hall and had to give him huge hug, as everybody else was... that's what you do when people get baptised, after all. He gave me the biggest grin ever and said he wanted to talk to me, then practically dragged me off to the kitchen, which was unoccupied.

He said stuff about how much he liked me and how well we'd got on recently, how much we had in common etc… Really didn't know what to do with myself, or what to say if he finally said something I had to respond to. Fortunately, he didn't. He wrapped up by saying that, despite all this, he wanted to apologise for coming on to me! He said that old habits die hard and, even tho he'd just got sorted with God, he was still on the lookout for someone to be with. As much as he likes me, he doesn't want a relationship right now… he wants to really get sorted with God, and give more time to his study etc.

Was lost for words. After a min or 2's silence, he just said, 'So, is that OK with you?' and I nodded, and we hugged…
just as O walked in, looking for the sugar.

He kinda turned white when he saw us, and dashed out again.

After a quick struggle for some appropriate words, where I thanked R for his honesty, and thought he'd done the right thing… I dashed out, in search of O.

Couldn't see him anywhere… Asked Fax, who said he'd gone home, as was feeling sick.

It was at that v moment that I knew, I KNEW, what I had to do… and who I wanted to be with, most of all. I got R to drop me off at O's, when he'd said goodbye to the last person at the church door.

O looked surprised to see me, but kinda pleased at the same time. We talked and talked… about Pete, about his mum, about God… and about us.
And I told him.
And he said it was the best decision I'd ever made.
And I know it is.

Sat 12 Nov

An interesting week. Life is good. Had no idea things could be like this, or that I could ever feel so… so 'sorted'. Not in a definitive kinda way, more in an 'on the right tracks at long last' kinda way.

Have found out the truth re Libs n Fax. Accosted them on Mon eve, when Annie was all over, and they were hanging out in the kitchen together, with:

'OK guys… is there something going on between you 2 or not?' (There are some moments when subtlety is just not appropriate.)

Fax, in a rather school-teachery kinda fashion, gently led me to a chair at kitchen table and sat me down. Quietly, and with much control, he reported:

'Yes, Jude... there IS something going on between myself and Libs...

('Ha!' thought I. Knew it knew it knew it knew it!!)

We're good friends.'

Ah. Right. Perhaps I didn't 'know it' then.

Libs had hyena-style fits of laughter, while Fax explained that they WERE close, had lots in common and were enjoying each other's company etc... but had 'never snogged'.

Turns out that Libs DID sleep with that old bloke she picked up at Fusion, as she thought she was missing out on the lifestyle she'd pretty much 'left behind' since she came to Romania with us. She says she regretted it before he'd even left her room, and now KNOWS she wasn't missing out on anything... only regret.

After she'd explained all this, she asked if she could borrow some CDs from my room, and kinda dragged me off upstairs. As soon as we got to my room, she announced: 'Jude, I wanted you to be the 1st to know... I've done it! You know babe... sorted it all out with God n all that... become one of you lot!' MAN did we hug and cry! More emotional than all the weepy bits of *Annie* put together! Had a strong suspicion that she had something to tell me... she's never been a great fan of my taste in music!

Was great to come back downstairs and witness her telling everyone. Fax was a well happy bunny... he actually cried!

I insisted Jon do multiple replays of the bit in *Annie* where they sing 'Let's, go to, the mo-vieess!' Would love to be like Grace... chuck out all my trendy hipsters and don the elegant pale yellow dress she wears. Fab.

When I voiced this ambition, O said it would suit me... bless!

Sun 13 Nov

Just when we all thought this house would smell of poo forever... just as we were deliberating re putting up posters in each room for visitors saying, 'Yes, we know it stinks of poo and, no, WE DON'T KNOW WHAT IT IS!'

Love Jude

...the mystery has been solved!

Some bloke (looking rather like Einstein, hair-wise... not that I know what he looked like in person, but I must've seen pictures once or something) came a-knocking at our door this am, asking if he could 'retrieve his experiment'. Those of us who'd been congregating in the hall, preparing to go to church together, crowded round him while he explained he lived here last year, but had forgotten his science experiment when he left and now realises he needs it.

Einstein led the way upstairs, and we all followed, quite intrigued. He pointed to a small door underneath the airing cupboard door that, I must admit, I'd hardly noticed before, and had certainly never opened. He opened it up and reached inside...

We all yelled, 'Ahh-HAA!' (or words to that effect) as the effect of his experiment reached our olfactory organs, and reminded us greatly of the poo-like smell we've been suffering with since we got here. It was indescribable... like a sewer or something, but surely far worse! Oblivious to our reaction, he looked lovingly at his long-lost friend, and did begin to explain it to us... but we were outta there! Not sure if it was the word 'growth' or 'bacterium' that got me out the front door the fastest!

Been a bit busy this week with study.

No, that's not a joke... I really have! Is kinda hard, actually, ploughing through the text books and making sense of it all, but am gonna persevere. Have no choice. Is what God wants me to do anyway... he wouldn't have put me here otherwise.

Oh... hot goss... Duncs n Lauren are back together! Is all v confusing but, according to Mike, who had a whole bunch of us to lunch today, they HAD been feeling that it was all wrong to get married just coz of the baby. But, with a bit of counselling from their parents (and Mike), they have come to the conclusion that, yes... they shouldn't do it JUST coz of the baby... but it's not JUST coz of the baby... they'd been thinking about marriage anyway, and are totally up for spending their lives with each other, AND feel that God is totally for this.

Great! Wedding back on then... out with the bridal mags again!

Uh-oh... that reminds me... as b'maid, will have to be in loadsa wedding piccies... yuk. HATE having my piccie taken... always end up with double (sometimes triple) chin. Is prob hereditary as Dad has had double chin for

172

as long as I can remember… but then why doesn't ABBY have one, huh? Typical!

Mon 14 Nov

Post-*Mary Poppins*

Dick Van Dyke… unfortunate name, bless 'im.

Libs AGAIN whisked me off to my room during the mass game of Uno after the film. This time tho, she asked if I wanted to go to southern Spain for a week in the Xmas hols!

Wild!

Her dad is over there now (her parents have split up now) shacked up with some lass ½ his age, in a large villa… pool, tennis courts, staff… the lot. She hasn't spoken to him for 6 months or so, and feels it's time to 'do some sortin', whatever that means. Is all good tho. Will be a great hol… and not a timeshare apt in sight!

She's gone back downstairs now… I'm just filling you in before I rejoin the rabble! Oh Bob… you're so good to me. Talking to you is therapy in itself. Still, know now that it's talking to GOD I need to work on… and giving him a chance to talk back. Have felt well close to him this week. He's got me thinking more re the whole 'holistic mission' thingy… really think he's gonna use me to help people… perhaps he already has! Perhaps… ahh… Lydia's yelling up that it's my turn (in Uno game)… must dash…

Post-Uno Is so good to have so many mates here this eve… and now I DO feel like I belong, until I get to be with God, that is… till he comes back to take me home.

Amusing thing happened in lounge just now… Convinced that no one was watching, I took the opportunity to practise my 'goldfish exercises'. Confused? Well, Sas told me yesterday that, to rid oneself of a double chin, you tip your head back, then drop your jaw as if doing a huge yawn, then shut mouth again… and you need to do 10 repetitions of this per day.

Was ½ way between jawdrop 8 and 9, when Duncs said (for all to hear), 'Jude… what ARE you doing?'

At which point I just went as red as the wine that some of them were drinking. Sas saved the day by telling them all about the exercises (gee – thx, Sas)… but turned out that most of them considered themselves to be cursed with a double chin, and got stuck into their new exercise routine without hesitation. Hard to explain how rib-ticklin' it is to see a whole room full of people do exaggerated goldfish impressions… but, well, made me laugh!

Right… will get off back downstairs now… need to see O before he goes – need to know what time he's picking me up tomorrow… he's taking me for more driving practise. He really is amazing…

but then so's Fax, Libs, Sas, Lydia and… the list goes on and on. My mates. My wonderful, sometimes bizarre… and ALWAYS unpredictable, mates.

Is funny to think that am now a Singleton once more… but a contented one. This is right for me now. It's me and God all the way… HE'S the one I want to be with, most of all.

Wonder if that ½ tub of Ben & Jerry's (Karamel Sutra) in freezer will divide OK between the 20 or so people downstairs… Perhaps will just save it for when they've all gone. After all, like Dawn French would say, 'It's not Ben & Jerry's… it's mine!'

Arrrggghhhh!!! Sutra reference has now reminded me of something I MUST get on and do… return Oscar's sex books. Wish I'd thought of taking them to BURP bonfire the other night… that would've been an appropriate method of disposal! Still, are not my property… really need to track the guy down and relieve myself of them. Maybe, if I

Ahhh… am being summoned again… Reuben is yelling that if I don't come down PRONTO to take my turn, he'll eat my Solero.

What Solero? Has someone been on Tesco run and bought SOLEROS?!

Sorry, must dash – I have a higher calling…

Love Jude.

Love Jude is Annie's second novel, a sequel to the popular *Dear Bob*. She is married to Mark, and has two children – Tilly and Fraser. She is commissioning editor of *thewalk* magazine (www.thewalk magazine.com), and is studying for a degree in Theology by distance learning. She loves the Tube, bubble n squeak, *Friends*, and BOGOF deals!

For Bible studies relating to issues raised in *Love Jude*, and *Dear Bob*, and other information about the two books, visit

www.dearbob.com

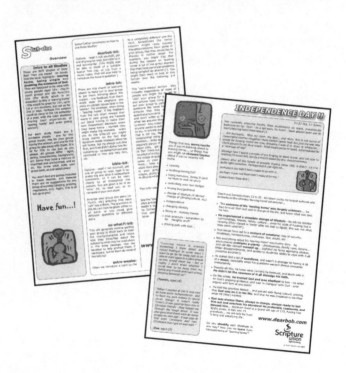